Forget Me Not

Forget Me Not

Amber Stokes

~Seasons of a Story~

ISBN-10: 061597600X
ISBN-13: 978-0615976006

Praise for *Forget Me Not*

"FORGET ME NOT is a beautiful and intriguing tale of love and forgiveness. Refreshingly real with characters whose flaws and struggles are both believable and easy to relate to. A solid foundation for what's sure to be an excellent series."

~ MOLLY EVANGELINE, Author of the PIRATES & FAITH series

"With a fresh new writing style and a unique historical setting, FORGET ME NOT by up-and-coming author Amber Stokes is a must-read. Set in Nevada's Virginia City, Elizabeth Lawson battles with the age-old quest for true love amongst the rough men that searched for their fortune in the rugged and untamed west. Stokes will surprise and delight you with the unfolding of relationships in this original and unpredictable historical romance."

~ SANDRA LEESMITH, Author of LOVE'S REFUGE

Praise for *Bleeding Heart*

"BLEEDING HEART is a moving tale of open wounds, desperately broken hearts, obsessions that derail multiple lives, and the love that heals all."

~ SERENA CHASE, Author of THE RYN and Contributor to USA TODAY'S *Happy Ever After* blog

"From first word to last, the characters, the story, the premise of Amber Stokes's debut novel captivated and intrigued me. This was no simple romance. BLEEDING HEART speaks to anyone who has ever loved and lost."

~ ELIZABETH LUDWIG, Author of NO SAFE HARBOR

"A tender, heartfelt story with a maturity and emotional intensity well beyond that of a debut novel, sure to please readers and reviewers alike!"

~ LAURA FRANTZ, Author of LOVE'S RECKONING

"BLEEDING HEART has a whole lot of broken hearts all over the place, except for the reader's—
a solid debut novel for Amber Stokes."

~ MICHELLE GRIEP, Author of A HEART DECEIVED

Dedication

To my Heavenly Father, for remembering me always.

*And to my grandma, my kindred spirit—you are not forgotten.
Love you forever.*

Psalm 25:6-7

"Remember, O Lord, thy tender mercies and thy lovingkindnesses;
for they have been ever of old.
Remember not the sins of my youth, nor my transgressions:
according to thy mercy remember thou me
for thy goodness' sake, O Lord."

Part I:

Tender Mercies

"Remember, O Lord, thy tender mercies and thy lovingkindnesses; for they have been ever of old."

Chapter 1

Clear Creek Canyon, Colorado
Summer 1885

Forgotten. The word echoed on the wind through the ponderosa pines, brushing across David's shoulders and thoughts in cold sweeps. He tugged his hat lower over his forehead and sank into his coat, letting Liberty lead the way home. His quarter horse weaved between the trees, her white and black splotches ducking in and out of dusk's shadows. David stroked the horse's neck, more for his own sake than hers. Her warmth and the creak of the shifting saddle took away some of the sting of the wind's whispers.

Forgotten. The word came on bursts of air like the pulsing smoke of a departing train. The feeling of being left behind was never assuaged. It didn't matter that he had forgotten once. They had forgotten him first and forever after.

Forgotten. If only it all was. But memories tugged at his collar and slipped cold deep beneath his skin.

Dear God, help me. The familiar prayer had barely risen in his chest before another plea caught his ear. He pulled on the reins and turned the horse's head, glancing to his left. Into the canyon. A scream rose again, and he thought of the freezing water that came off the mountain and formed Clear Creek, winding its rocky way below.

His heart seized as he directed Liberty toward the cliff edge, glancing down only to see how far the woman was before heading down the incline. Pebbles tumbled ahead of him, but he kept his gaze trained on her, trusting Liberty to get him to the canyon floor safely.

"Come on, girl—quickly now." He tried to speak with calm urgency, but he could hear the panic breaking his voice. When something scurried into the rocks ahead of him, he startled, and Liberty slid forward a little with a whinny of fright. "It was probably just a pika. We're all right." But not so for that woman in the river if he didn't get to her in time.

When they finally reached level ground, he sent Liberty into a near-gallop, his heartbeat slamming through his chest like the echoes of Liberty's hoofbeats through the canyon. The trail he'd taken had brought him out not too far behind the woman, and he quickly closed the gap.

"Hold on!" He slowed slightly as he dug his hand back into his saddlebag, rummaging around for the rope he kept there. He finally grasped it and tied one end securely to the saddle horn, trying to complete the task quickly for fear he would lose the woman if he looked away too long.

Gathering up the rest of the rope, he pushed Liberty harder. His eyes scanned the rapids, fear drowning out all sound until he saw the woman's head reemerge closer to his side of the river, dark hair plastered to her face. As a breath filled his lungs again, he glanced ahead. The terrain would turn rocky soon, which would make it harder to follow the woman.

As soon as Liberty had surged forward far enough, he sent the loose end of the rope flying across the river. "Grab the rope!" he yelled as loud as he could. Could she hear him? "Listen to me. You've got to grab the end of the rope!"

She turned toward him—right before she slammed into a rock.

He jumped off of Liberty and stumbled forward, barely catching his balance before tossing Liberty's reins over the nearest sturdy branch and tying them with shaking hands. Then he took hold of the rope still tied to the saddle and splashed into the river. The white water roared, dulling the clamor of long-ago memories. As soon as he caught sight of the woman again, he dove, trying not to think about anything but saving her.

The rocks had slowed the woman's progress, but they had also taken any remaining fight out of her. She wasn't trying to get to the surface.

The frigid, frothy water pushed him toward her. He closed his eyes against the rush, but they flew open when he felt her hand, a mere second before the water plunged him under. Lunging forward, he caught hold of her arm and pulled her up with him. They both gasped as they broke the surface.

Digging his fingers into her arm with his one hand, he clung to the rope with his other. She went under again, and he panicked. How could he use the rope to climb out to safety with only one hand? He yanked her up until he heard her gasp, then pulled her as close as he could while yelling, "Hold onto me!"

She met his gaze and nodded before throwing her arms around his shoulders, clinging desperately as he brought his other arm around to grab onto the rope.

His body jolted as the rope stretched to its full length. He imagined Liberty bobbing her head in agitation and only hoped he had tied the rope and reins tight enough. Slowly, hand over hand, he fought against the current. The mountain runoff ran right through his skin as if he were nothing but a ghost.

Long, frozen moments passed before he threw himself face-first onto the rocky shore, the woman still clinging to him. He lay there, breathing in and out, feeling her breathe with him as she lay on his back. Despite the chill that had buried itself deep within, a warmth went deeper still, knowing that she was all right, that they were breathing together.

13

Finally, he rolled to his side, causing her to slip down next to him. He glanced over her. *She's hardly a woman.* She appeared so young, thin and trembling next to him. But a second thought flowed right after the first. *She looks familiar.* A few freckles crowned the bridge of her nose. Her spring-green eyes regarded him with awe, or was that just shock?

She suddenly pushed herself up with her hands and coughed up water, spasms shaking her slight frame. He sat up and touched her back, waiting. When the coughs died down and her body continued to shake, he stood. Coiling the rope as he went, he untied it from the saddle horn and stuffed it into his saddlebag, exchanging it for a blanket. Liberty whinnied, and he touched his forehead to her neck. "Thank you, girl."

After a minute he lifted his head and looked at the girl. She stared at the creek as she trembled, and he thought that perhaps it was from more than the cold. Perhaps it was the way her fists were clenched instead of rubbing her arms, or the way her head was lifted at an almost defiant angle. He found himself hesitant to approach her—until she glanced back at him. Her eyes held fear, and when he walked toward her, she melted. Her shoulders drooped, her head fell into her hands, and she began to cry.

"Hey now." His voice was as gravelly as the creek bottom. He tried again. "It's all right." Kneeling beside her, he touched a hand to her back again. The sobs traveled up his arm and made his heart ache. "You're all right now. Everything will be fine."

Water spattered over his nose just as he uttered the words. Tilting his head back, he saw dark clouds had gathered. A summer storm was brewing.

Rain poured faster and harder. Covering the girl with the blanket, he then held his hand out to her. She looked up at the sky and back at his hand, her face wet from the creek, the rain, and her tears. As soon as she grasped his hand, he tugged her over to Liberty. "My cabin's not far from here."

He swung into the saddle and pulled her up behind him. But when he noticed that she was fumbling with the blanket, he quickly slid down. "Scoot forward. You can sit in front of me." She nodded and did as he asked while pulling the now-damp blanket firmly around her, for what little good it would do. Best to get to the cabin as soon as possible.

He climbed back on and wrapped his arms around her to grab the reins. She leaned into him, and a fierce and familiar protectiveness welled up. He would bring this girl home safely.

A rumble of thunder seemed to originate inside her, rolling through Elizabeth until her head snapped up and her eyes sprang open. She must have dozed off. Shivers attacked her as she glanced around at the ponderosa forest they were passing through. A stand of aspens surrounded a cabin up ahead, but she found her gaze drawn instead to the hands gripping the reins in front of her. She studied the scrapes on his knuckles. The hair on the backs. The faint lifelines of blue flowing down them. Those hands had helped her out of the river, and up onto her feet. They weren't overly large—just big enough to fit around her own. Strong enough to do the job. Gentle enough to comfort her. Just…enough.

Another round of thunder boomed, and she jumped.

"It's all right. We're almost there." His voice rumbled through her just like the thunder, and she felt heat rise to her cheeks.

As soon as the man reined in his horse in front of the porch, he jumped down to the ground and held those hands out to help her. With a face that felt as red as the anger that had driven her out of town, she attempted to slide down off the creature on her own, still clutching the corners of the blanket at her throat. But her legs were ready to fold like paper, and when her feet touched the dirt they sent her sprawling into the man.

"Whoa." He caught her by her arms, speaking to her as kindly as he did his horse.

She didn't want kindness tonight. She wanted an excuse to let lose all of the emotions raging inside of her. But as she opened her mouth to tell him she didn't need his help, she met his gaze. The calm, understanding brown reminded her of how home used to be, and in the remembrance's wake the anger broke away and the weariness washed in. Her shoulder hurt from where she had hit the rock. Her head ached, and her legs were sore. Without really meaning to, she let her head drop to his shoulder.

"Come on, then. Let's get you inside."

He bent down and swung her up into his arms. Her head remained on his shoulder, and she sighed in gratitude as he carried her over the threshold and into the shelter of the cabin. When he set her on the bed at the back of the only room, she whispered, "Thank you."

He lingered with his face close to hers for a moment before taking the wet blanket from her and stepping back with a faint smile. "So you do talk. That's good, because I have a lot of questions."

She cringed. Just what she didn't need.

Apparently noticing her reaction, he added quietly, "But not tonight."

With a grateful nod, she slowly peeled off her boots, pulled back the quilt covering the bed, and climbed beneath it. Thunder rolled over the cabin and took her exhausted mind beneath the waves of sleep.

David lay awake in his bedroll, stretched out in front of the stone fireplace that graced the wall at the end of his bed, where the girl now slept. It had been so long since anyone else had been in this cabin. Not since the man who had practically raised him, Frank, had passed away six years ago.

He picked at the dirt on the floor, wondering how the girl had fallen into the creek, why she had been out this way, and who she was. The rain continued to pelt the roof with as much force as it had assaulted him and Liberty when he'd brought the horse around to the large lean-to on the side of the cabin hours before. He hoped he had patched up the leak well enough and she had enough hay.

Rolling onto his back, he groaned. His body ached, and he could only imagine how much more the girl was hurting. Something about her presence made him restless. The cabin had always been suitable for his needs—large enough to live in comfortably, quiet enough to suit his desire for solitude. He considered himself a simple man who needed nothing more than God, Liberty, his gun and traps, and a town nearby for anything he couldn't hunt or make himself. It was the way Frank had taught him, and Frank had seemed content. Of course, Frank had always said his life was more interesting with David as his "son." And now, David discovered a craving he never knew he had for something interesting, for someone else to be a part of his life again.

He sat up and looked at the bed. The girl's face was turned toward the center of the room, and in the dim light from the fire he could see her hair had dried to a reddish-brown color, wisps falling across her face like strips of bark. She looked so small in his bed, lying there like a misplaced piece from his childhood.

"Where did you come from?" Lifting his head to the ceiling, he continued, "Why is she here, God? What do You want me to do?" The restless feeling only grew at the harsh sound of his own voice amid the *pops* of the fire. Deciding he wouldn't get any sleep tonight, he stood and walked to the stove at the front of the cabin. He would make flapjacks.

He cringed as the cupboard door creaked when he reached for the flour, and as the pan knocked against the stove. How quiet was quiet enough not to wake a person? He didn't remember.

When the first flapjacks were cooking in the pan and he had cracked some eggs for scrambling, he turned and found the girl watching him from where she was still lying in the bed. "I'm sorry I woke you."

She gave a small, lazy smile in response, and his heart stopped.

"It's all right." She pulled the quilt closer and added, "May I…may I have some?"

Glancing back down at the food on the stove, he grinned. "I was planning on giving it all to the horse…"

He waited a beat before glancing back over his shoulder. Her brows were lowered in confusion. But when she met his gaze, her eyes brightened and she shook her head with a chuckle.

The laughter was an echo from happier, louder times. He pondered what else he might say to get the same reaction from her, but nothing witty came to mind. He should have spent more time in town, visiting with people, learning jokes, hearing stories. But the solitude of the mountains always called him back. As soon as he talked to someone, he longed to come home. Until now. Maybe it was because this girl, for some strange reason, made his home feel—well—even homier.

"Were you actually serious? Because those flapjacks will only be good for the horse if they burn any further."

Her words startled him, and he realized with chagrin that he had forgotten to flip the cakes. They were a dark brown, far darker than the girl's hair. He shook his head in an attempt to clear his thoughts and slid the flapjacks onto a plate, preparing to fix some more. Her second round of laughter was worth the blunder, though.

"What's your name?" he asked suddenly, tired of thinking of her as "the girl."

She remained silent as he put some new, lighter flapjacks on a separate plate for her. He turned and brought it across the room, and she watched him, wariness written on her features.

"You don't have to tell me." *But I wish you would.*

She sat up and reached for the plate. "Elizabeth." Her eyes studied him. "What's yours?"

"David."

He went back and got his own plate, then pulled up a chair a few feet away from the bed, giving her room but wanting them to eat together. When she still didn't start eating, he realized she was waiting for something. "Do you mind if I say grace?" he asked, pleased when she nodded in consent. "Heavenly Father, thank you for this meal, and thank you for bringing us out of the creek. Please watch over us during this storm, and help me get Elizabeth home safely. Amen."

"Amen." She dug her fork into the eggs and started eating with abandon. He hid a grin behind a bite of flapjacks.

As curious as he was to learn more about her, he waited until she had finished everything on her plate before asking, "Could you tell me how you ended up in the creek?"

The cabin felt too small to hold all of Elizabeth's uncertainty. How could she explain what had happened when she had hardly absorbed it all herself? She glanced around at the four close walls, the autumn-colored quilt with the leaf designs, the empty tin plate in her hands—just not at the man across from her. She bit her lip, afraid of the silence, but afraid to break it with her story. Would he think she was silly? Would he understand how important all of this was to her?

Before she could brave a word, she felt the plate gently tugged out of her hands. She stared at the hard-packed dirt floor and listened to the water being pumped and then sloshed around as David washed the dishes.

"I fell in."

"I guessed that much." His tone teased a reluctant smile from her.

"I found out I have a brother."

Peeking up, she saw his eyebrows scrunch, but he didn't say anything.

"My parents died from the scarlet fever when I was little, and our neighbor took me in. My older brother had apparently gone west before I was born. My ma—the woman who raised me—she told me about him a few days ago after talking with a friend whose husband was heading out to Nevada. I just don't understand why she had never told me before. And she never even told my brother about me."

Her words gushed forth like the rapids in Clear Creek Canyon, and she found herself twisting the quilt in her hands, once again too worried to meet David's gaze. So she just kept talking.

"I was angry. I mean, he's my brother by blood! I should have known about him, should have had the chance to write to him, to go meet him. He's all I have, and he doesn't even know I exist." Tears misted her eyes, and she shook her head in frustration. "I couldn't stay in the house. We live outside of Golden, and I just…ran. I've been out here for a couple of days, I guess."

She heard a clatter and jumped. He must have dropped a dish in the basin.

"You've been wandering around in the canyon for a couple

of days?"

She couldn't decipher the emotion in his voice beyond the surprise, so she rushed on before he could clarify it. "I've been trying to figure out how to proceed. But I…" Oh, this was embarrassing. A blush burned her cheeks. "I was getting frustrated. I went down to the creek for a drink, and as I got up I kicked a rock and slipped. Then you found me." Thankfully.

He was silent. She could only imagine what he was thinking. *Foolish girl, to get so upset over something so trivial. You could have died, all because you let your emotions carry you away! Why don't you think before you act?* Somehow, the voice in her head had transformed into Sarah Anne's. Her ma must be so disappointed in her. *Isn't my love enough for you?* She could hear the breaking in Sarah Anne's voice, and tears burned hotter than her blush. She loved Sarah Anne. She just wished her ma understood how much this meant to her—how the years without an older brother now ate at her, and how she didn't want another year to go by without meeting him. *Jacob.* It was just right. A sturdy, kind name.

"Here."

She broke out of her thoughts and saw that David was holding out some sort of jerky to her. "Venison," he explained. How did he know she was still so very hungry? She took his offering and gave him a grateful smile.

He sat down next to her on the bed, a respectable distance away. "Did you ever figure out what you were going to do next?"

She yanked off a bit of the jerky and chewed a moment before responding. "I have to go meet him. I haven't figured out yet how I'm going to do that, as I don't have any money, but I'll find a way."

"It's that important to you?"

His voice was strong, serious. She turned to him, clutching

the jerky in her hands, surprised to find him regarding her with determined compassion. Like the look Mr. Vance, the owner of the general store, always offered her when he asked about her and Sarah Anne as he gave her a little extra of everything she ordered. Mr. Vance was such a nice older man that she had secretly taken to thinking of him as her grandfather.

Redirecting her thoughts to David, she raised her head and gave one short, certain nod. "Yes. I have to know…" She shrugged. How could she go on without meeting that piece of her past, that piece of her parents, herself? Jacob had answers. And she had to have them.

With Elizabeth's nod, David's path was set. Or perhaps it was when she had said she'd been wandering aimlessly around in the canyon, desperate to come to terms with the news of her brother. Or maybe it was that sense of familiarity that wouldn't quit nagging at his soul.

He clasped his hands together and worked his jaw. "Where?"

"Where what?"

"Where is your brother?" He waited, sensing a journey.

"Virginia City. In Nevada."

The bed creaked as she shifted, and the sound spurred his mind into a race. Virginia City, site of the Bonanza strike. A mining town hundreds of miles away. But didn't the Overland Route—the transcontinental railroad—go right through there? He remembered the route from the older newspapers Frank kept around and read to him.

He got to his feet and paced, finally kneeling down next to the fireplace and stoking the flames. Was this girl determined enough to try to get to Virginia City on her own? She would get herself killed if she continued to wander around in the mountains alone.

But what if she ended up going home and getting her mother's help? Maybe the woman was for Elizabeth like Frank had been for him. Maybe she would understand.

And maybe she wouldn't. Not all parents cared. Not all families went to great lengths—or any lengths at all—to make sure every member was counted. Remembered.

He shoved the poker against the fireplace as he stood. Elizabeth startled, her expression wide-eyed and anxious.

"I'll take you." His announcement was punctuated by the *thump* of a log shifting in the fire.

Her frown seemed to pull her eyebrows down. "What?"

"Tomorrow. If the storm's died down, we'll leave for Virginia City."

She twisted the quilt in her hands, obviously pondering his statement. With pursed lips, she cocked her head. "Why?"

He shrugged his shoulders and shifted his weight, his heart also shifting from a feeling of rightness to one of disquiet. The fire within burned brighter and snapped louder in response. He had to find out who this girl was. He had to reunite her with her family. He had to get out of this cabin.

"Well?"

She jumped up and pulled the quilt back again, glancing at him as she did so. "If you're really willing, then yes, you can take me. I'll repay you someday. I promise."

Before he could wave her words away, she added, "But promise me we won't go through Golden." She crawled into the bed and yawned.

The transcontinental railroad went through Wyoming Territory. Cheyenne, to be exact. They could meet the railroad there and travel straight through to Reno, not far from Virginia City. So they'd travel the Rockies north a ways. Maybe not the easiest plan, but it would give him time. For what, he wasn't sure. To get used to the thought of leaving these mountains? Or to come to terms with these new feelings that were melting his common sense along with the walls that usually blocked out the past?

After he checked the stove and tossed the blackened flapjacks out the door for the raccoons, he returned to the fireplace to find Elizabeth's eyes were still open, but barely. She was waiting.

"We'll skip Golden," he finally agreed. She gave him the satisfied smile of a little girl who had been told she'd get to ride a horse the next day. And she would. He smiled softly at the thought and watched as her eyes drifted shut.

With stiff limbs, he climbed into his bedroll for the second time that night. As he fell asleep, change permeated his dreams like the smell of rising bread, growing into a mass that might consume him and alter previous ideas and plans, or blow them away entirely, like a passing cloud on the horizon.

Chapter 2

ELIZABETH WOKE to the sight of an empty cabin, and fear clawed at her heart as she sat up and took in the details of the room. David's bedroll was gone. One of the cupboard doors was open, and there was nothing behind it. The room seemed hollower than it had before, like there were other things missing she just couldn't place. Had David abandoned her? But why?

Then she realized that the fire was still burning. He could have simply forgotten it or left it going as one last gesture of kindness. But somehow the crackle of the flames on the logs reassured her. He would return.

She placed her stocking-clad feet on the cold dirt floor and wrapped the quilt around her shoulders. Standing in front of the fire, she pushed worries about Sarah Anne away, opting instead to wonder about her brother.

Was he a miner? Maybe he had found some silver, enough to provide for them to live comfortably as a real family. *He might already have a family of his own.* The thought of little nieces and nephews only made her smile, though. She would have a big family.

Of course, Sarah Anne had said Jacob might have moved on from Virginia City. It had been nineteen years after all. But surely someone there would know where to find him.

The door suddenly opened, and Elizabeth spun around. She squinted at the bright rectangle of daylight silhouetting David.

"You're awake," he said.

"You're here," she replied with a smile. He was going to

keep his promise. He was going to take her to her brother.

"I've just been gettin' things ready. The only thing left to pack is you."

He walked with purpose toward her, and she laughed. "Are you just going to throw me over your saddle, then?"

"Something like that." He stopped in front of her. His brown hair brushed his ears, like it had been a while since it had been trimmed. But his face was freshly shaved, and she was glad for it. His chin and cheeks deserved to be shown off instead of covered behind a beard. Her own cheeks heated at her wayward thoughts.

"I'll just put your bed to rights, then."

She turned to set the quilt back on the bed, but he put a hand to her arm. "Just fold it up, and we'll take it with us."

With a nod, she proceeded to do as he asked while he went to put out the fire.

When she had run her fingers through her hair and grabbed the items David asked her to gather, they went outside and shut the door behind them. As they walked through the dewy grass, around the cabin to the lean-to, she asked, "What about your cabin? Will it be all right while you're gone?"

She glanced over at him in time to catch his one-sided smile. "I don't think it will go anywhere, if that's what you're asking."

She shook her head and smirked.

"If someone needs to use it while I'm away, I don't mind."

He led Liberty out of the lean-to as Elizabeth stood waiting, holding the supplies. "What if someone takes it over? Will you—will you fight them for it?"

He laughed. "Fight for it?" Taking the items from her one by one to add to the saddlebags, he gave her another smile. "I doubt it would come to that. I doubt many people will come up this way, anyway. But who knows what the next few weeks will bring?"

Indeed.

"You ready, Elizabeth?" He held on to the horse's bridle. The question carried an underlying weight she didn't want to consider, so she didn't respond. She pulled herself up onto the saddle, her legs to one side, and he swung on behind her. They set off across the mountains together.

The early afternoon sun burned away the remnants of the storm as they rode through the foothills. As they headed down into a summer-browned valley, patches of wildflowers spread out before them. David felt the tension leave Elizabeth at a rapid pace as she leaned back against him, and his heartbeat picked up a similar stride.

"Are you hungry?" He was sure they could both do with a meal and a chance to stretch their legs.

"Food would be lovely." She sighed, and he smiled.

He reined in Liberty by a grassy spot with some reddish-orange flowers, pointy like the spikes on a brush. Jumping down, he turned and helped Elizabeth. His hands felt as hot as the color of the flowers where they touched her waist. As soon as her boots grazed the ground, he dropped his hands and busied himself with retrieving some jerky and crackers from his saddle-bag.

When he turned with the food, he found her kneeling in the flowers. Her fingers hovered over the blossoms, and a slight smile touched her lips and lingered. Carrying the food over, he hunkered down next to her, moved by the awe and innocence in her eyes as she intently regarded the blooms.

"They're so beautiful."

He nodded, not trusting his voice.

"It's as if they're on fire. Like little torches." Her smile bloomed fuller. "I almost feel I could be warmed by them."

A very real heat spread through him as he watched her. He picked a small yellow flower and handed it to her with a piece of jerky and a handful of crackers. She took it all from his palm and sat back on the grass, her eyes alight with such a simple joy.

It reminded him of something.

"How old are you?" he asked as he also sat back and bit into a cracker.

"Eighteen." She must have detected the skepticism in his gaze, because she added, "I'm telling the truth! I turned eighteen two months ago."

In May. She hardly looked a day over sixteen, let alone two months over eighteen.

Remnants of a memory yanked at his mind. "What's your last name?"

"Lawson." She dusted the crumbs off her hands before leaning back. The girl was quick when it came to making her food disappear.

Elizabeth Lawson. How old would she have been? Five. With two brown braids, a sweet round face red from running after him, and green eyes bright like mellow light shining through leaves. She had looked at him just the same then, when he handed her the forget-me-nots, as she did now, among these flowers. His breath hitched at the final release of a memory that had been teasing him off and on over the years, every time he came across blue flowers.

"David?"

He blinked and focused on this more mature, beautiful—but still young and sweet—version of that little farm girl. "What?"

"I think I lost you for a moment." She picked at the grass, and he studied her while she was looking down. *Not lost. I've found you.* It was too soon to share his full story, as he was still tracking it like a deer or mountain lion, following the subtle marks left on its trail. But it felt so good to have this piece back. *Thank you.*

Her light voice called him back again. "How old are you? You never told me." She tilted her head as she waited for his response.

"Twenty-one."

"Huh."

She stood, and he followed suit. "What?" he asked, curious.

"You're not so much older than me."

As she walked back to Liberty, she glanced back at him with a little smile that sent warmth straight through him, as if the flower torches had set him ablaze.

Elizabeth waited for David to help her down from Liberty when they came to a good spot to make camp for the night, next to a stream and not far from the treeline. She appreciated his kindness, in the little things, in the very big things. As he set her on the ground, she looked up at him and whispered, "Thank you. For being a gentleman. For"—she shrugged— "everything."

Part of her wanted to ask why he was doing it. Sarah Anne would surely disapprove of her going off with a stranger, no matter how kind he seemed. She winced. Sarah Anne probably thought she was dead.

The only response to her words was a nod, before he said, "I'm going to gather some wood for a fire. Will you set up our bedrolls?"

She nodded, too, and heaved an inward sigh of relief at the mention of more than one bedroll. She didn't think he was the kind of man to make her share one with him, but as Sarah Anne would have pointed out, she knew nothing about David. So why was she trusting him? As she patted Liberty, the answer was clear. *Because he's my liberty. My freedom to do what I need to do.*

The breeze found her between the ponderosas, and as the cold hit her, so did a question: *Do you feel free?*

She shook her head. It was a silly thought. Her emotions were all over the place lately. What did it matter how she felt about this path?

You know true freedom. Walk in it.

Liberty nickered and stamped a hoof. "It's all right, girl," Elizabeth crooned. *Right?*

She tried not to worry about her plan as she set out the bedrolls across from each other, with a space between for the fire. Shivers racked her body, and she straightened and rubbed her arms.

"Are you cold?" David's voice startled her, and she turned to see him coming from the wooded area, some sticks of varying size in his hands.

More than you know. But aloud, she only said, "A little."

"I'll get this fire going in a hurry," he assured her, but his smile was enough to start warming her.

She sat on her bedroll, watching him build the fire. The first flicker of flames cheered her, and as he turned to her in the dim light, she met the shadow of his grin with one of her own. He wasn't a huge man by any means—rather thin, but with enough muscle to show he could handle living off the land. But as he stood to his full height, it felt like he towered over her. He didn't scare her, though. More like he made her feel safe.

After he handed her some more crackers and jerky, he settled on his own bedroll across the fire. "I promise I'll catch something fresh for us to eat tomorrow."

"I don't mind this. Although I wouldn't mind something else, either." She blushed.

He laughed. "Alrighty then. Maybe I can get a rabbit."

She nodded, distracted. Never mind food. She had too much for her mind to chew on. Like what she was going to do about the guilt that had started to eat at her.

"Care to talk about whatever's causing you to frown so deeply?"

Her gaze flew to his over the flames. This man had prayed over their meal last night. He had saved her from the river, and he was helping her to find her brother. And he was the only one around to talk to.

"I'm worried about my ma."

He stretched his hands out to the fire but remained silent.

"I shouldn't have left the way I did, I know, despite everything." The confession felt good, like something that had been stuck in her throat dissolved. "Do you think she'll come looking for me? I don't want her to get hurt. She wouldn't know where to begin to search…"

She jumped when David shot to his feet. He ran a hand through his hair, and she waited, wondering.

"I've got to get more wood." He cleared his throat. "But maybe when we get to Cheyenne you can send her a telegram. Let her know where you are and what your plan is."

He turned and walked away before she could respond. Crossing her arms over her chest, she listened to the crackle of the fire, shivering again. He'd come back.

Chapter 3

DAVID SPOTTED what he wanted near the shrubs up ahead and grabbed the shotgun he kept on the back of Liberty's saddle. Elizabeth had opted to stay by a small river they came across earlier in the evening, but David was determined to bring back some fresh meat. The rabbit would be perfect.

Tying Liberty's reins to a tree, he gave her neck a pat and then approached the bushes carefully. When he was sure he couldn't get any closer without startling the creature, he slowly lifted the gun to his shoulder. *Deep breaths. Focus.* The hunting would keep his mind off their conversation of several nights before. No more talk of families. Just this rabbit. Just this source of food.

The bullet found its mark, and he grinned. He walked the remaining distance and knelt down to grab the rabbit, pleased by its size.

Suddenly, a scream caused his head to snap up. Rising with the rabbit dangling by its legs from his grip, he searched the woods, getting his bearings. *Elizabeth.* He hadn't wandered far from where he had left her, but whatever the exact distance, it was too far. *I never should have left her alone.* Sprinting to Liberty, he untied the reins and swung on with his gun beneath his arm and the dead rabbit on his lap. He pointed Liberty toward the river and spurred her on. "Come on, girl. Faster!"

Please don't let it be too late. Please be with her. Please help me save her.

The trees rushed by. As soon as the blue ribbon of water unfurled before him, his vision narrowed. Just the river. He had to make it in time. Elizabeth couldn't die. His life—his past, his future—had been stretched too far by her appearance. If she disappeared, there would be no going back. *No going back.*

The clearing in between the trees grew wider, until he was there. He jumped off of Liberty, tying her reins to the branch of a tree at the edge of the forest. Still holding the rabbit and gun, he took in the situation.

Elizabeth was standing by a thimbleberry bush, cowering before a black bear standing on all fours. Not much older than a yearling, but still a good size. It would be new to being on its own. Hungry. Startled by Elizabeth's presence. And possibly angry.

"Elizabeth," he called, "don't cower! Stand tall. Tell him to go away."

"This isn't funny, David." She was crying, and his gut twisted as he walked toward her and the bear.

"I know, Liz."

The bear grunted and stood on its hind legs. Elizabeth screamed again, falling backward. David's heart stopped as Elizabeth curled into a ball and the bear took a swipe at her side. David fired a shot into the air, causing the bear to fall to its feet and turn to him. Raising the rabbit's carcass high, he made sure the bear could see it before he threw it several feet away from the bear—and Elizabeth.

The bear sniffed the air and then lumbered over to the rabbit. David made his way to Elizabeth, hoping the bear would be satisfied. Hoping they could get away safely. Kneeling down next to Elizabeth, he glanced over her, satisfied her injuries weren't too serious, but concerned over how pale and silent she had become.

"Here." He handed her the shotgun, which she took with trembling hands. Then he lifted her into his arms. Peeking at the bear and seeing it tear at the rabbit, he sighed and walked back toward Liberty. Elizabeth hid her face in his shirt.

When he got to the horse, who was tossing her head back and forth, he set Elizabeth down and slid the gun on the back of the saddle among his other possessions. Then he untied the reins, climbed into the saddle, and pulled Elizabeth up in front of him. With one last glance at the bear, busy with consuming the food, he urged Liberty forward.

Elizabeth leaned back against him, and he pulled her closer, feeling the shaking of her shoulders against his chest. As they rode through the woods and into another clearing, the first stars glimmered in the vast, dusk-yellow sky above, emphasizing their vulnerability. All he could think about was how he had almost lost her. *Thank you*, he whispered to God. She fit so well on his saddle, with his arms around her. He couldn't let her go.

David's horse's name was a joke. *Liberty.* Independence and freedom were illusions from the past as Elizabeth was forced to realize her dependence on David. Without him, she might have died—drowned in the creek, killed by a bear. Without him, she would never make it to Virginia City. She knew that now. But knowing the truth of her situation didn't erase the sting she felt at being so helpless. Wherever David led her... wherever he decided to go...she had no choice but to follow. No choice.

She shook from the remnants of fear, from the birth of a new anger.

"Please let me down." His arm was holding her tight against him, brushing painfully against her hurt side. She was lassoed like a horse. Captured.

"I think we should put more distance between us and the bear before we stop," David replied, dismissing her plea.

Fine. She would command him to let her go.

"Let. Me. Down."

"No." He was unwavering.

Feeling sick, she tried to pry his arm loose. Her breathing became shallower, and her heart beat faster than a gallop. She would beg, if that's what he wanted.

"Please. We've gone far enough. I want off this horse."

"Elizabeth..."

"Please!"

Pulling back on the reins, David finally let her go. Jumping down, Elizabeth could barely get her legs to support her, and she cried out at the fire in her side. But within a moment, she was running—as far from David as she could go.

"Where are you going? Elizabeth!"

She knew he was following her, and she hated the feeling. But there was nowhere to go. Nowhere she could run, except into the pines, which was too frightening of a prospect as night descended. So she turned to face him, and he practically plowed into her. He grabbed her arms to steady her, worry written in the lines on his face.

"What is this about? I don't understand."

No words would tell David what she wanted to communicate to him. Without thinking, she lashed out at him, pounding on his chest, scratching his face.

"I detest you! And I will not go one more mile with you. You will not control me!"

At first, David's shock allowed her to get in a couple of good blows. But just as soon as she was sure she was going to mar his handsome face, anger—white hot like the stars above, contrasting with the calm night—filled his eyes, and he grabbed her wrists with a force that both surprised and scared her, yanking her close.

"Do you honestly think that I've been tryin' to control you? To force you to go with me?" He shook her, and Elizabeth winced, flames crawling up her side and down her arms. "I just saved your life! I didn't have to come with you on this reckless journey. I could have let you leave my cabin, free to wander aimlessly and starve or...be eaten by a bear." The blood drained from her face at the thought, but he wasn't finished. "You aren't familiar with this land like I am. I've only wanted to help you. To protect you. Don't you understand?"

"I never asked for you to come! You suggested it yourself."

Elizabeth cowered, sure that the back of the hand David raised would make contact with her face. Instead, he shoved her, causing her to fall to the dirt. She clutched her side and scooted backward.

With her display of fear, the heat that had roared to life in his eyes melted into icy shock. But the power of the fire had already left its mark.

What is happening? David blew out a breath, lifted his head to the twilight sky, and closed his eyes. His arms shook, and his eyes burned behind his eyelids, threatening to embarrass him further. Yet it wasn't embarrassment that hit him when he looked back down at Elizabeth. It was shame. Horror. What was he doing?

"Elizabeth." Her name tasted sweet, tempting, like forbidden fruit. She held knowledge—of his past, of his home. She made him feel powerful, helping him remember, helping him forget. Helping him to see things he had never seen before.

But at what cost?

He took a step toward her, and she retreated, her face turned away from him, her skirts stained by the grass and dirt.

"I'm so sorry."

His gaze was drawn to her side, and it hit him that she was still hurt. He had added to her pain.

A groan seeped from his lips as he stumbled forward and

fell to his knees beside her. "Let me see." He held out a tentative hand, afraid she would stand and run. Her eyes remained on the ground, but she removed her hands from her side, letting him see the torn bodice. The scratches weren't deep, but when he pulled back some of the material to examine the wound, she winced, and he cringed in response. Though the sun was almost gone, there was enough light to see a large bruise forming, the skin red, but only a few long lines showing drying blood. The bear must have just hit her, trailing his claws rather than digging in. Probably more frustrated than determined to kill.

Standing, he called Liberty to him and rummaged through the saddlebags until he found some bandages. Taking them and his canteen, he knelt back down and cleaned the scratches, then wrapped her side for protection. He worked as quickly and gently as he could, but by the time he was through Elizabeth was shivering violently.

He grabbed an extra shirt from his bag and helped her direct her arms through the sleeves, then buttoned it up for her. Each little button took forever to obey him, and his own hands trembled with a strange fatigue as he buttoned the last one near her neck. His fingers lingered at her throat as their gazes finally met. She swallowed, and he brushed back her tangled hair from her face, longing to make things right between them. "Please forgive me," he whispered, the words haunting the air between them like the ghosts of his past.

She fiddled with the top button, biting her lip as she glanced back the way they had come. Where they had left the bear behind them. "I'm sorry, too," she finally said, so low her words seemed an echo of his own. "I didn't mean to lash out. I just... I'm so..." She hung her head.

Reaching out, he grazed her soft chin with his finger, finding a smile. "I know. It's been a difficult journey so far." And it could only get harder. But he wanted to do this. He had to.

Chapter 4

THE NEXT MORNING was gray, and Elizabeth wondered if another storm was coming. She was still reeling from the one that had crackled last night between her and David. Hugging her knees close and tucking her hands inside the sleeves of the shirt he had let her borrow, she waited beside the cold ash that used to be their fire. She didn't want to wake him up. Didn't want to disturb him, afraid of what the sleeping bear might do if riled.

Even as she thought it, though, she didn't think he would truly hurt her.

How long until the sun would clear the clouds away? The hazy morning was making her homesick. What she wouldn't do to be sitting at the kitchen table beside Sarah Anne, with a hot cup of tea and some sugary cakes to munch on. Yet there was little comfort in the thought, not when she longed for those things so desperately, and not when the guilt chomped on her conscience. She was dead to Sarah Anne. She had to be.

David stirred, a moan escaping him as he sat up in his bedroll and ran a hand through his messy brown hair. A grin touched her lips. He looked like a little boy woken from his nap.

"What?" He smiled in response to her amusement, and just like that, the remnants of their storm dissipated.

"Just thinking what a cute child you must have been." As soon as the admission left her mouth, a blush rushed up her face. *Foolish!*

His own face paled, a marked contrast to the color in hers. Was he concerned about her forwardness?

"Tell me about your childhood." He sounded genuinely interested, albeit quiet. She blew out a breath of gratitude for the diversion from her silly remark.

"Well, I don't really remember much about my parents. Sarah Anne's the only family I've really known, although we've always been close to our neighbors." She smiled softly at the thought of them. "There are two girls not much younger than me. Let's see... Louisa is sixteen, and Christy is fifteen. And Amos is nearly twenty-three."

Staring out at the blue sky peeking through small tears in the clouds, she confessed, "You know, I think Amos is one of the reasons I really want to meet my brother."

"Why's that?" David's voice sounded gruff, scratchy.

"Amos is a great big brother. I guess I've been sort of jealous of Christy and Louisa, that they have him around all the time. I can't believe I truly have a big brother of my own." She couldn't hide her excited grin, but it faded when she glanced up and saw David's expression. "What's wrong?"

He shook his head. After a moment, he rose and declared, "We should keep moving."

A part of David filled with questions, begging for release. A bigger part couldn't stand to hear any more. Rage turned the morning sky as red as a foreboding sunrise, although he knew it truly remained as gray as his family's apathy.

He wasn't surprised Elizabeth had no memory of him. She was only five when he disappeared, and it must have been not long before her parents passed away. That would be the tragedy she remembered. What had he been to her?

Once, he had been a friend.

Once, he had been part of the neighbor family she held dear.

Once, he had been the one to put a smile on her cherub cheeks with a fistful of forget-me-nots.

His eight-year-old self had brimmed with pride, though he hardly would have admitted it to Amos or any of his school chums. That last summer before the accident, he had spent afternoons running with Elizabeth in the fields. Her squeals whenever he got close enough to touch her arm had him laughing uncontrollably, and they often ended up lying on the grass giggling and guffawing together.

The last time they played chase, though, Elizabeth talked him into picking flowers before they had to return home...

"You have to promise not to tell Amos. Or any of my friends. Or even Louisa or Christy. Promise?"

Elizabeth stared at him thoughtfully, her brows scrunched and her head cocked. "Boys are silly," she declared, still rooted to the spot on the creek bank, determined to get her way.

"You have to promise, or I won't do it." He crossed his arms, straightening his back to emphasize his height, and thus his age.

The sunlight teased her brown hair, and he tried to hide his grin at how mussed the braids had become. The top of her head looked like a bird's nest, or a rat's. Then he frowned as he wondered if he'd get blamed again for bringing her home in an "unladylike condition," as their mothers called it.

"All right," she agreed as she shook her head. "I promise. Now let's go!" She tugged on his hand in an attempt to drag him over to a patch of little blue flowers.

"If I find out you snitched, I'll never play with you again." He bent to pluck some stems, his threat only half-hearted. The thought of never spending time with Elizabeth left him feeling lonely. Amos did stuff with him, but his older brother seemed to prefer playing with his group of friends. His younger sisters were too little, and more interested in playing with dolls, anyway. Elizabeth was the only one who really seemed to want his company. If her continued

admiration meant picking a few flowers, he could handle it, as long as it remained their secret.

Elizabeth paid his words no mind. She pulled up the flowers by their roots and lovingly held the dirty lengths of them in her hands. He smiled. And she thought boys were silly.

After a few minutes, he extended his handful of flowers to her. Her green eyes lit with delight as she added them to her bunch.

"My ma calls those forget-me-nots," he told her. "See how they have little yellow suns in the middle? And the petals are blue like the sky? Ma says they help us remember sunny days and stuff." He still didn't fully understand why it mattered, but it made him feel smart to tell Elizabeth about their name. She probably didn't know anything about them.

Her eyes widened as she regarded the flowers in her grip. "That's a long name." She tested it out. "For-get-me-nots. Forget-me-nots."

He laughed. "Yeah. That's what they're called."

"I won't forget." She giggled at her own joke.

He smiled. "Good. Race you back to my house!"

In the thrill of the game, the flowers were forgotten, dropped somewhere in the fields.

But David was comforted to realize that the memory re-mained.

Elizabeth helped David pack up their bedrolls. He was so quiet, lost in something she wasn't privy to. At least he grew calmer with every moment that passed. She had been worried that the tense look on his face as she talked about her neighbors would lead to another fight between them. Why he should get so upset about talk of her family and friends didn't make sense to her…well, maybe it did. He had to be lonely living by himself in the mountains. He probably just hated dwelling on the things he missed.

As her heart constricted, her mind went flying off with an idea. Maybe David and her brother would become friends. Maybe God had brought her into David's life to give him a family, of sorts.

Thoughts of God made her bow her head as she patted dirt over the ashes of their fire. *Forgive me. Guide me. Please. I know I went about this all wrong… But I am grateful for David, confusing emotions and all. I'm just so sorry for hurting Sarah Anne.*

If Sarah Anne even cared that Elizabeth was gone.

Elizabeth shuddered and stood, leaving the buried ashes behind as she hurried over to David and Liberty.

"Are you ready to leave?" he asked.

She nodded. *More than ready.*

He lifted her onto the saddle and swung on behind her. As he urged Liberty onward, she asked on a whim, "Are you ready?"

"It seems a little late to be asking that."

She chuckled, almost feeling his smile hovering above her head.

"No, I mean, are you ready to get to Wyoming Territory, to Cheyenne?"

His arms seemed to tighten around her, and she found she didn't mind the sensation.

"I think I will be, when we're there."

Another chuckle bubbled up her throat, but didn't find release. There was a seriousness in his tone that begged for her understanding. She squirmed, waiting.

He continued, "I've never left Colorado. Never left these mountains. In a way, I relish the thought of seeing what else is out there, but this is still home."

She started to agree, just as he added, "And I—"

They both stopped, silent. She bumped his arm. "Go ahead."

42

"I was just going to say that I don't mind this."

"This?"

"I'm in no hurry to end our adventures. I haven't had so much fun since I was a boy." Teasing laced his tone.

She grinned as she was rocked side to side in the saddle, Liberty's movements sure and steady. "Who said our adventures will come to an end when we get to Cheyenne?"

A blush followed her words. Amos would lecture her good for being so bold with a man. Although she had a feeling he would get along well with David if they ever met.

David's laughter set her at ease. "True. And we still have time before we get to Cheyenne anyway."

Leaning back against David, riding Liberty, she decided she wouldn't mind if it took a very long time to get to Cheyenne.

Chapter 5

THEY ARRIVED IN CHEYENNE much sooner than David would have liked. He wondered if he was ready for what awaited him, as Elizabeth had asked him several days ago.

Earlier in the day, after he had made sure Elizabeth was settled in her own room in the hotel, he didn't think he'd been ready to face selling Liberty. But he'd done it. While turning his four-legged companion's reins over to the livery owner had torn out a chunk of his heart, the thought of his childhood companion waiting for him, depending on him, helped fill in the gaping hole.

Now he walked down the hall to her room, hesitating at the door.

One knock. Then two. Just as his heart started racing in concern, she pulled the door open wide and gave him a smile that pushed his heart over a cliff and then gave it wings to fly.

"Elizabeth, you look beautiful." She wore a new green and gold calico dress he'd purchased for her. The colors made her eyes glow and the reddish tint in her brown hair shine. Everything about her radiated light and joy, rendering him helpless to turn away.

When they were little, she had been sweet and fun, but also a nuisance at times. He never could have imagined back then that he would be the one desiring her attention. It was as if they had only taken a short break from the games of chase they used to play, and now he was back to following after her.

She bit her lip and looked down at the floor, an adorable

pink spreading through her cheeks. "Do you like it? The dress, I mean." She performed a twirl for him and then peeked up at him, uncertainty in the angle of her face.

If you could only see my thoughts, little Liz, you'd never have to worry. But *he* would. Perhaps it was best she couldn't see the things that went on in his mind—his secrets, his fears, his unworthiness. If Elizabeth had been old enough to remember him, would she still have forgotten him, too?

With a jolt he realized he had taken too long to respond to Elizabeth's question. Her lower lip trembled in the low light of the lamps in the hall, confusion clouding her clear green gaze.

Reaching out to cup her chin, he declared in a husky voice, "The dress is lovely. *You* are lovely."

The clouds in her eyes scudded away, and her smile returned in full glory. "Thank you for buying it for me."

He liked how she didn't offer to repay him. She was a little girl who had been given a gift that made her happy, and her simplicity and innocence warmed him. He would see to it her sweetness remained protected.

When he offered his elbow, she took it, beaming up at him. He escorted her down to the hotel's restaurant, relishing her chatter about the train trip they would begin tomorrow and what her brother might be like. The more she talked about her brother, though, the more serious she became.

After supper, he brought her outside and walked with her down the street. The wooden sidewalk creaked beneath their boots. Elizabeth had turned quiet, staring at the craggy gray mountains. David, on the other hand, couldn't take his eyes off her.

"What's wrong? And don't tell me 'nothing.'"

Her mouth closed as quickly as it had opened.

"It has to do with your brother," he declared. Noticing a board sticking out above the rest on the sidewalk, he gripped

Elizabeth's hand in the crook of his elbow and guided her around the tripping hazard. She didn't seem to notice the detour, though, as she kept her gaze steady on the horizon.

"You can tell me," he urged.

She shook her head. "You'll be angry," she finally whispered.

His hold on her hand tightened. "Why?" A foreboding settled on his shoulders like the darkness of the descending night as he awaited her response.

Would David stay with her if she told him? Elizabeth hadn't meant for her worry to be so obvious to him, but it was like the guilt was dragging her features down and her thoughts far away. *Guilt...*

"Oh my goodness! I was going to send my ma a telegram." She glanced around wildly, looking for a telegraph office.

David gently grabbed her arm and redirected her gaze to him. "You can send the telegram tomorrow before we leave. The office has to be closed by now, anyway. Tell me what's bothering you about your brother."

She heaved a sigh. "Promise you won't leave me?" She knew it wasn't fair to ask that of him, but the thought of him abandoning her in Wyoming Territory and returning to his cabin in disgust and outrage made her eyes fill with tears.

His brown eyes softened, and he caressed her arm with his thumb, creating a heat she could feel through her sleeve. "I won't leave you."

Her heart lightened, and she confessed, "I don't know for sure my brother is in Virginia City. Or Nevada, for that matter."

His eyebrows pinched, and he let her go. She shivered at the loss of his touch.

"What do you mean?" He crossed his arms, waiting. A

man stepped between them on his way to the saloon behind them.

"I mean that, when I was a baby, that's where my brother went. To Virginia City. But I suppose he might not necessarily be living there anymore…" She trailed off. The heat had jumped from her arm to his eyes. *Oh, dear.*

"So the last time anyone heard of his whereabouts was when you were a baby? Eighteen years ago?"

She gave a hesitant nod.

"Elizabeth! He could be anywhere by now. He could have left the country for all we know. The Bonanza strike has long since passed, and he most likely moved on." He paced, and she followed his movements with her eyes. Despite his obvious frustration, she wasn't afraid. He had promised her, and she trusted him to help.

She brushed his sleeve with her fingers, causing his gaze to shoot to hers. "I'm sorry I didn't tell you before, David. But surely someone there would have known him. There are old-timers in every town, people who settle and know of the comings and goings. Someone has to know about my brother."

"Not necessarily."

She ignored his doubt. "He might even still be living there." Letting the longing show in her eyes, she stared at him and added, "It's the only place I know to check. The only way I can try and find him. Please forgive me for hiding the details. Please go with me."

Tears stung her eyes again as another man jostled her and gave the two of them a rough look before disappearing into the saloon. David's arms fell to his sides, and he sighed before placing one hand at her back and leading her the way they had come, to the hotel.

"Of course I'll go with you."

She dabbed at her tears with her sleeve and smiled in relief.

They would go to Virginia City together.

The next morning David stood outside the telegraph office, listening to the faint but sweet sounds of Elizabeth's voice as she talked with the operator. He glanced in the window and saw her bent over a small piece of paper, writing her message and laughing at something the man said. When she walked out a few minutes later, her shoulders seemed lower and her head higher.

She came to his side and took his arm. "I know I should have sent word to Sarah Anne long before now. But it feels good to let her know our plans."

He squeezed her hand and gave her a smile as they made their way to the train station. Behind his smile, though, a battle between guilt and jealousy raged.

They arrived at the train station, tickets in hand, a few minutes before their train was scheduled to depart. Boarding the train was like taking a final step away from all that was familiar—the family that had forgotten him, the cabin in the Rockies, and even his childhood memories of Elizabeth. Now was the time to let it go. To make some new memories.

As the engineer gave a loud shout of "all aboard," David took one last look at the town of Cheyenne through the window. The rocky peaks framing the town were intriguing, but not as intriguing as the idea of what lay ahead for them. While the future was still so mysterious, especially with the uncertainty of Jacob Lawson's exact location, he knew one thing: he wasn't going to just step out of Elizabeth's life as soon as he handed her over to her brother.

Soon the train rumbled to life again and continued its journey westward. They would take this train to Reno, Nevada, and then they would take the Virginia & Truckee to Virginia City, where they would hopefully find Elizabeth's brother, or at least discover where he might be. Again, David found himself in no hurry for another leg of their journey to end.

Sitting next to Elizabeth made his heart race nearly as fast as the train—if not faster. Her excitement spread to him, making his own knee bob in a display of nervousness. Reaching over, he held his palm out to her. Without hesitation, she placed her hand in his. His chest tightened at her tender touch, and a prayer rose in him. *Thank you, God, for bringing us this far. Please continue to go with us.*

Part II:

Transgressions

"Remember not the sins of my youth, nor my transgressions."

Chapter 6

DAVID WAS GOING to buy a pistol and holster the first moment he could get away. He knew it would be a necessary expense—could sense it as soon as the train pulled into Virginia City. The clang of machinery, remnants of the mining equipment still being put to use, hardly covered the sounds of trouble roaming the streets: angry shouts, saloon music, and pounding hoofbeats. Even years after its heyday, Virginia City appeared to be full of life…and danger. Apparently, not everyone had given up hope that there was still silver yet to be discovered in the hills surrounding the town.

"Here, let me give you a hand."

Turning swiftly, David saw another young man, with blond hair, blond beard, and tan skin, offering his hand to help Elizabeth down the steps of the train.

"Thank you." Elizabeth's smile to this complete stranger made David's blood boil hotter than what he had heard of the air at the bottom of the mines.

"The name's Joseph, ma'am. But you can just call me Joe."

Enough was enough. Who did this man think he was? Stepping down right after Elizabeth, David went to stand beside her, gripping her elbow firmly. "And why would the lady need to know your name?"

Joe gave David a curious glance, but no malice filled his light brown eyes. In fact, David detected a glimmer of humor in them.

"Can't say as I blame you for askin'. If the lady was just

any lovely lady stepping off the V&T, I would simply help her down and tip my hat. But I was just walkin' past when I saw you both…and I just noticed somethin' familiar about her."

David doubted that. More like Joe was walking past when he was struck by the sweet face of his innocent Elizabeth.

Joe turned to Elizabeth. "Have you ever been to Nevada before?" His grin was a mile wide, and David felt a growl rising in his throat. Why did he ever go along with Elizabeth's foolish scheme? He should have kept her far away from places like this, where men like this preyed upon gullible ladies.

Elizabeth's smile hadn't dimmed. "No, I've never been out this way before. My brother has, though. His name is Jacob Lawson."

Joe stepped back in apparent surprise, his mouth opened slightly and the hat he had swept from his head earlier crushed against his heart. "Jacob Lawson?"

Elizabeth nodded, eagerness causing her to bounce a little on her toes. "You know him?"

If Joe's smile grew any bigger, it would reach his ears. "I work for him! He owns the general store on C Street. He never spoke of a sister, though."

Elizabeth's expression fell a little. "That's because he never knew of me. I was born after he left home."

"I see." Joe offered Elizabeth a wink, and then—finally—glanced at David. "I'll be happy to take the young lady to Annabelle. That's Jacob's wife," he added for clarification.

David's face burned, most likely redder than a freshly painted stagecoach, by the feel of it. *Can Elizabeth truly be falling for this?* A glimpse at the joy lighting her gaze answered that question.

Before he could give a response to the no-good woman-stealer, Elizabeth declared, "I'd love to go meet my brother's wife, but I'd prefer that David come with us." She blushed, but continued, "David made sure I arrived here safely. I'm sure my brother would consider him an honored guest."

David stood taller as he stared hard at Joe. Perhaps the man would hear what Elizabeth wasn't saying: the two of them were inseparable. And no friend of her brother, no matter how friendly he seemed, was going to swoop in and change that. If Joe was even telling the truth, which was very unlikely.

Joe simply maintained his smile and said, "Of course."

A whistle and a rush of air caused David to turn in time to watch the train roll through a tunnel on its way to the rail yard. When he spun back around and caught Joe staring unabashedly at Elizabeth, he couldn't help but wonder if his own life was headed for a dark, consuming hole.

Elizabeth was intrigued by the sights and sounds of her brother's town, glancing all around as she and David followed Joe up the hill from the train station. Virginia City was a busy place, consisting of people who were still trying to strike it rich. Whether that wealth came from within the surrounding hills or from others with both needs and vices, it didn't seem to matter. And while Elizabeth didn't really feel the pull of money, she did thrill to the excitement in the air, desiring possibilities she had never dreamed of before. If ever there was a place for a new start and new opportunities, Virginia City was it.

But the surroundings weren't all that intrigued Elizabeth. Joseph—"Joe"—was like no one else she had ever met. She guessed him to be young, certainly not much older than David. But he had a certain agelessness to him, enhanced by the beard and his rather long hair. His words were gentle, but his demeanor exuded both humor and a hidden knowing. If her brother was anything like Joe, she was even more eager to meet him.

Letting her gaze swing upward, Elizabeth was stunned at the steepness of the mountain they climbed. The lure of silver must have made these people stick like burrs to the hillside, refusing to tumble down into a valley of poverty and failure. If it wasn't so exhilarating, Elizabeth might have thought it to be utter foolishness. As it was, she found it thrilling to walk up the steep streets. Surely there was no other town like this in the world.

"Jacob lives on A Street, but he spends most of his time in town," Joe said over his shoulder as he led the way up the partial alphabet of streets. Shaking his head, he added, "I don't know how Annabelle can stand being alone in that house so much. She'll be glad to have another woman around fer company." Joe offered her a smile that warmed her. But the warmth quickly died away when she saw the scowl on David's face as he walked beside her. There had been something different about him ever since they had stepped off the train, and Elizabeth didn't like it. Why wasn't he affected by the excitement of this town? She had seen him angry, hurt, sad, confused…but now he was just plain grumpy.

Her breathing growing labored, she huffed a question for Joe. "Is my brother short on funds?"

"Naw, not at all. He's doin' fine. I think the fire of '75 really struck fear in him, though, ya know? So many people lost everything. He had to rebuild his business, but he still had his home. Decided not to give up and move on." He nodded his head. "I really admire him for that. It takes courage to rebuild. And now look at him! He has a wife, plenty of money, and a thriving business."

Joe paused, then added in a quiet voice, "With a decade

separating him from that disaster, ya would think he would finally feel secure."

Elizabeth pondered Joe's words. Joe probably thought Jacob worked too hard. Maybe her brother got that from their father. Not that she really remembered what her father was like, but many farmers had the same trait.

Shaking her head, Elizabeth craned her neck again and squinted at the mountaintop. It continued to rise above them, a tan habitation full of secrets. "What is this mountain called?"

"Mount Davidson. But that's its official name. I prefer 'Sun Mountain.' That was its first name."

"Sun Mountain," Elizabeth repeated, liking the way the name matched the hill's golden color. "I think it fits better, too."

Joe sent another smile her way. "Reckon yer right."

Joe found himself looking back more than was safe, and he wished that David-fellow didn't stick to Elizabeth like flapjack batter to a frying pan. Jacob was a good friend of his, and he figured that any family of Jacob's would be good, too. He just never could have imagined *how* good.

"Where do you live, Joe?"

Another question from Elizabeth, but he didn't mind. In fact, he wished she would never run out of questions. Of course, judging by the look on David's face, Joe guessed David was wishing the opposite. That brought a grin to his grimy face—a face he knew would be cleaner during Elizabeth's stay than it had been for years. He'd make sure of it.

"Well, ma'am, I live out of town a ways, in the canyon."

"Oh. But didn't you say you work for my brother here in Virginia City?"

"Yep. I stay at a boardinghouse in town during the week,

then head back home come week's end."

"Who watches your home for you while you're away?"

"My brother. He and I both work a ranch down there in the canyon. Well, mostly my brother and some hired hands do the work now. I help out when I can."

"Why would you work in town when you have a ranch?"

Joe looked back and gave her a wink as he replied, "Wouldn't want to miss all the fun in town, now would I?"

When Elizabeth blushed and glanced down at the ground, he returned his gaze to the street. "My brother's the eldest of us two, so the ranch rightfully belongs to him. I would move into town, but I really do love it down there. So I make my living up here and get my rest, so to speak, on the ranch. And only the Lord knows whether I'll have to someday make a choice between the two. Until then, I'm as content as cattle grazing on green grass."

"Which is rather scarce around here," David mumbled.

Joe smiled wide. "You noticed that, too?"

When he arrived at Jacob's house, Joe waited for Elizabeth and David to catch up. David seemed to be doing fine, although a noticeable drop of sweat slid down his forehead. But Elizabeth was breathing heavy, and her face was red from the hard walk. Joe wanted to ask if she was all right, but David kept very close to her and didn't seem agreeable to anyone else doing the same.

Elizabeth must have spotted the look of concern on his face, as she hurried to reassure him. "That was quite a walk, but I needed to stretch my legs after all that time on the train." She smiled, and the temperature seemed to spike several degrees. Nodding, he led the way up to the front door and knocked.

Annabelle answered the door right away, the constant lines of melancholy still etched on her face. Her gaze took in the newcomers, and she turned to Joe with new lines of confusion wrinkling her brow. "Who did you bring?"

Elizabeth stepped forward, her smile only slightly dimmed. She held out her hand. "I'm Jacob's sister, Elizabeth. It's so wonderful to meet you."

Annabelle gasped. "Jacob's sister? I didn't even know he had any siblings." Not waiting for an explanation, she bypassed Elizabeth's outstretched hand and gathered the girl up in a hug. "I'm Annabelle."

Joe grinned, sensing a friendship forming. Good. The Lord knew Annabelle needed a friend.

The smile that had grown on Annabelle's face faded when she looked past Elizabeth to see David. "And may I ask who this is?"

"Oh! This is my...uh...dear friend, David. He made sure I got here safely."

Annabelle nodded to David. He removed his hat and replied, "Ma'am." Well, at least the man had manners for everyone else but Joe.

Joe cleared his throat, and Annabelle stepped out of the doorway, motioning for all of them to come in. "I wish Jacob could have been here to greet you, but he should be home later today."

While he doubted Elizabeth or David caught it, Joe didn't miss the skepticism in her eyes. And he couldn't blame her for it, either. The contrasting innocent delight in Elizabeth's green eyes—clearer than her brother's—was all the motivation he needed to say his farewells and head straight back to C Street. He was going to give Jacob a piece of his mind...and maybe his fist.

Chapter 7

A FEELING OF DREAD pulled hard on David, making him wish he could back out of the house like Joe had done and return to the train. He had done what he set out to do, which had, surprisingly, turned out to be easier than he had thought after Elizabeth's confession back in Cheyenne. He'd delivered her safely to her brother's home. Yet, even if he could somehow find the will to step out of Elizabeth's life, something felt amiss, and he wouldn't let her suffer through any unknown trouble alone. He couldn't.

Maybe, just maybe, when he had figured this problem out, she would be willing to leave with him.

Sensing that someone was directing a question at him, he focused his attention back on the ladies gathered in the small parlor. "What was that?"

Annabelle repeated, "Will you be able to find someplace to stay? I'm so sorry that we don't have enough room for you both, but…"

"It's fine." That was that, then. He would search for a room and a job. Shouldn't be too hard.

Turning, he noticed Elizabeth's expression had fallen. Her brows scrunched as she bit her lip. "You're not staying?" Her whisper quavered in the air between them.

"I'll be around. I won't leave you."

"You'll tell me where you'll be stayin'?" It was a plea.

"Of course."

Taking one last look around, David admired the room with the small, colorful chandelier, furniture with soft blue cushions, flowered wallpaper, and deep burgundy carpets. Elizabeth would be comfortable here.

"Well, I'll be going now." He regretted the uncertainty in Elizabeth's soft, sagebrush eyes, but he walked out the door and let it shut firmly behind him.

Joe leaned against the counter of the general store and glared at Jacob Lawson. "When are you going to realize that people need you? And I'm not talkin' about here." He waited for Jacob's inevitable denial of the truth. Jacob couldn't seem to tear himself away from his work, not even to focus on his wife or his best friend. At least, Joe fancied himself to be Jacob's best friend. He hardly knew anymore.

"I know." Jacob turned away from the shelf where he had been stacking cans of beans. "I just can't believe that I have a sister. That she's here. I'm not ready to face her yet."

"You can tear yerself away from yer business for a few hours, can't ya? Don't ya trust me enough to take care of things while you're gone?" Joe wouldn't admit that he was glad he was the one to find Elizabeth at the station—and that he wouldn't mind spending more time with her. Let Jacob stew for a while and suffer for his stupid choices.

"Of course I trust you. There's just a lot I need to take care of here. You know it's hard for me to get away at any time."

"Oh yes, I know. Whenever I see Annabelle I'm reminded of that little fact. You don't even have time for yer own wife, so how are ya goin' to find time for yer sister, right?"

Jacob's face turned hard. "Don't start with me. I have my problems, but I'm a good man. As your boss, I treat you fair, right? And Annabelle hasn't ever wanted for anything."

Shaking his head, Joe replied, "Except fer some company. She never wanted for that before you married her. How do ya expect her to handle the loneliness now?"

"Come on, Joe." Jacob sighed. "It takes a lot to make a living in this dyin' town. You should know that by now."

Joe couldn't deny it. Grabbing a can of beans off the shelf, he studied it, wondering how he could convince Jacob to do right by his sister. She had come all this way to meet her long-lost brother, and now he was being a stubborn mule of a man. That pretty little girl deserved better than this.

"Don't put her off for too long. She had to have sacrificed a lot to come here. No matter what sort of guilt yer feeling, she needs you." Tossing the can to Jacob, he shook his head. "Right now I'm on her side, and I don't see that changin' anytime soon, regardless of our friendship."

Jacob held the can tightly in his hands, staring down at it as if all the solutions to his problems were contained in that worthless piece of trash. Disgusted, Joe went to the door, ignoring the curious glances of customers.

Turning back one last time, he met Jacob's gaze and added, "At the rate yer goin', yer life won't be worth more than that can of beans." With that, Joe walked out the store and left his sorry excuse for a friend behind.

"What an interesting place to live!"

Elizabeth couldn't satisfy her curiosity quickly enough to suit her. She somehow needed to convince Annabelle to go into town with her and show her around. Not that sitting for a little while after that long, arduous walk uphill was objectionable. And visiting with her sister-in-law was certainly enjoyable. She hadn't talked to another woman since… Well, it had been a long time.

"It is a different sort of place, isn't it?" Annabelle offered a small smile, appearing amused by Elizabeth's enthusiasm.

"You have such a lovely home. I had no idea my brother was so...comfortable." Elizabeth admired the small parlor they were sitting in, eager to see the rest of the house and, eventually, the rest of the town. "Would you mind if I take a look around?"

"Not at all. I'd love to show you our home." Pride filled Annabelle's voice as she ran a hand down her long blond hair. Just the words "our home" seemed to lift her spirits. Elizabeth grinned. How wonderful that her brother's wife was so excited about the life she and Jacob were building together.

As Annabelle showed Elizabeth around, her excitement grew. There was the small kitchen with floral print paper covering the walls. The table was small but elegant, and the space was larger than the kitchen she and Sarah Anne had at home. Upstairs were the bedrooms—two of them. One was for guests, where Elizabeth would be staying. The room was done in greens and browns, and Elizabeth found it quite elegant with a large dresser and matching wardrobe.

Annabelle and Jacob's room was grand. The walls boasted red-and-gold-striped wallpaper, and a red carpet covered the floor at the foot of the bed. But it was the bed itself that really captured Elizabeth's attention. It was so big! Elizabeth admired the carved headboard and striped spread that matched the rest of the décor.

"This is magnificent." Elizabeth looked about her in awe. "Why, this might be even better than a room in a hotel!"

Annabelle's laugh was full of merriment. "I wouldn't think so, but I do love it. Jacob spared no expense." At those words, the laughter left her lovely blue eyes.

As they headed back down the narrow stairs, Elizabeth asked, "Would you show me the town, too? I know I just got here, but I can't wait to see more of it."

Annabelle shook her head. "No, I don't think that's a very good idea. Virginia City is still a rather rough town, even though there's good society here, as well."

Elizabeth cocked her head, noticing for the first time that Annabelle's speech seemed to be rather slow. It wasn't that her words seemed uneducated. It was more like each word was chosen carefully. Looking up to find Annabelle watching her, she scrambled for something to say and ended up returning to her plea. "Oh, but it would be so much fun! And we'll be going together, so we should be fine, right?"

Once again, Annabelle shook her head, not quite meeting Elizabeth's gaze. "I'm rather tired, aren't you? Why don't we wait here for Jacob to come home?"

"Well, I guess if you don't really want to go to town, maybe I could just venture a quick look around by myself." Elizabeth thought her eager countenance would coax a smile from Annabelle, but instead, she frowned.

"Elizabeth, I really don't think…"

"Oh, don't worry. I'll be careful, and I won't be gone long." Before Annabelle could protest further, Elizabeth rushed outside. Surprised at her own boldness, she turned back around to stare at the closed door. Since when had she become so fearless? And since when had she become so rude? Elizabeth pressed on downhill, afraid that if she let herself stop and really think she would be overcome by a disappointment she couldn't quite comprehend.

Chapter 8

AMAZING HOW HAIRY a man could get when there wasn't a woman around to impress. Joe looked up from the hair on the wooden floor and smiled at his image in the mirror, admiring the barber's work. "Do ya like the mustache, Bill? Or do ya think I should just get rid of it all?"

Bill took a step back and grabbed his chin with a finger and thumb, thinking deeply. "I think the mustache suits you." A slow smile crept up his dry and weathered face. "Besides, yer already shocking enough as it is with so much hair gone."

Joe grinned broadly. "And really, I look almost—what's that word?—uh, debonair, right? Like a gentleman." It was tempting to purchase new clothes to match his new look, but he didn't have that much money to be tossing about to the wind. The shave and haircut would have to do. His blond eyebrows fell over his eyes as he wondered what Elizabeth would think.

"You'll be impressin' every woman in town with the new Joe. They'll wonder where the handsome stranger came from."

"Just what I wanted to hear." Placing some money in Bill's hand, he added, "I'm headin' out to show the town of Virginia City the cleaned-up me."

"Have a good time, son." Bill waved as Joe stepped out the door and glanced up and down C Street. The middle of the street was crowded with people milling about and horses and buggies trying to weave through the herd. The saloons were open, but he knew the small groups of people inside would grow as soon as the sun began to set. Joe had never really had much desire to enter the Bucket of Blood, the Delta, or any of those establishments, but he knew that they were frequented by many of the citizens of this town. His ma's teachings still held sway in his life, and he was accountable to his brother, so he did his best to stay out of mischief. Too bad he couldn't say the same for Elizabeth's brother.

Stepping off the wooden sidewalk and out into the dusty street, Joe was startled to see Elizabeth wandering around, glancing into shops and practically running past the saloons. What was she doing out here all alone? Nervousness twisted through him, and his pulse picked up speed. He couldn't recall feeling such concern for someone else before, besides his ma, and he wasn't sure he liked the feeling. Like it or not, though, he was going to catch up to that girl before she got herself into a heap of trouble—and before she found herself on the wrong street.

It was the last job in the world David wanted, but it seemed like the last job in the world available to him. At least the pay was good. Actually, it was more than good. But then, was it really a wonder miners had to be paid so much to go into the depths of the earth and suffer all day?

As he headed out the office door, a fellow miner came up and started walking with him toward the mine's entrance. The man appeared to be Irish, and David was reminded again of how many different countries the miners represented. It was as if people from all over the earth had come to dig some sort of future out of the heart of the West.

"Where ye stayin'?"

It was the question that had been on his mind ever since he had left Elizabeth with her brother's wife. "I don't know. Why do you ask?"

"I'd rather die with a friend than an enemy, if it comes to that when we're down below. Jest wanted to do a good turn for the newcomer and tell ye to stay with me Cornish friends. Up near the top of Sun Mountain." The man shrugged. "They're not the fanciest or cleanest, mind ye, but ye go where there's cheap room, right?"

David paused and stared curiously at the man. "They live at the top of the mountain?"

"The highest streets." The man pointed upwards.

"Ah, I see." The higher levels of the city. "Must be some view from up there."

"Yes, indeed. They've got a grand view o' the valley."

"Mind if I ask why you chose to come here?"

The man now pointed to the ground. "Down there is me chance for a better future. Ye must feel the same, if yer here."

Nodding, unwilling to explain further, David resumed walking and then ducked beneath the wooden beams framing the mine's entrance. He picked up a pack with the equipment he'd need, just where his new boss said it'd be, and hefted it over his shoulder. A sudden apprehension seized him as he thought of going down into the mine. Returning to their previous topic, he asked the man, "Do you think the Cornish would accept me?"

"You're white, aren't ye?"

David preferred to ignore the wealth of prejudice in the man's tone. "But I'm not one of them."

"Talk to Mee-gall—that's what we call 'im. He'll help ye. He's a good friend." His words were simple, but full of gratitude. David liked the sense of camaraderie between the miners. *Although this must make it that much harder when one of them is lost forever in the darkness of the earth.* He shuddered.

"Come on." The miner led the way, and David had no choice but to follow. "It's time for us to give the others a break. Can't be down there for too long."

David could only imagine why, but soon he would know for sure.

Elizabeth was sure someone had called her name. Turning to scan both sides of C Street, she frowned. No one looked familiar, and the only person who knew she was in town was Annabelle, who apparently had no desire to leave the house.

Giving the busy dirt road one more glance, she gave up and continued her walk. Maybe she would recognize Jacob's store, even though she had no idea what it looked like. Surely a quick peek inside each shop would be enough to spot her brother. Her heart would recognize him. Unless he was in a back room, or on a break, or…

"Elizabeth!"

There it was again. Maybe someone was looking for a different Elizabeth. There had to be more than one Elizabeth in a town this big, right? Shaking off the bit of fear that had gathered around her mind, she came to another street heading downhill. Should she go a little farther? It did seem to be getting darker, which was disconcerting.

Suddenly, a hand landed on her shoulder. She screamed as she came face to face with a man she had never met.

"Elizabeth. What are ya doing here all by yerself? Don't ya know it's dangerous?"

The rapid beating of her heart slowed to a gentle pound. "Joe, ya startled me." Squinting up at him, her forehead creased. "Why, you look so different! What happened to your beard?"

One corner of his now-visible mouth lifted. "Do ya like it?"

Tilting her head, she studied him. Without thinking, she raised her hand, but she caught herself before she actually reached out to touch his clean-shaven cheek. Blushing wildly, she turned her face away, and said, "You look very nice."

Joe's laugh was hearty. Elizabeth glanced up, unable to stop her smile. Her gaze met his, and she was sure her face glowed redder than a flaming hot poker as she stared into his brown eyes, the color of golden soil. Homesickness rushed over her, and once again she turned away.

A gentle hand came to rest on her upper back. "You okay?"

"Yes," Elizabeth replied quietly. Her response could barely be heard above the din of the town.

"How 'bout I take ya back to Jacob's place?" Offering his elbow, he added, "It'd be an honor, ma'am."

The fire in her face descended to her heart, and she swallowed, ignoring his proffered arm. "Do you think I'll get to meet my brother anytime soon?"

Joe sighed. "If he listened to me at all, he'll be home before dark."

"Did you speak to him today?"

"Yes."

Satisfied, she allowed Joe to place her hand in the crook of his arm.

As they walked back down C Street, Elizabeth found herself continually glancing at Joe, longing to catch his gaze once more. Then a realization startled her more than seeing Joe without his beard. The reason she really yearned to see his eyes again was because they reminded her of David's. Of course, David's eyes were a bit darker, like the hills surrounding Virginia City at dusk…

The rest of the trip back to the house, she refused to look at Joe again.

Chapter 9

"ARE YOU MYGHAL?" David stood in front of the boardinghouse, ready to do just about anything to find a place to put up his feet and sleep. Never had he been so tired, so dirty, and so sore. He wouldn't get paid nearly enough for the pain working in the mines had already caused him. And the fear. Man wasn't made to work in temperatures like that.

"I might be. Depends on why ya be askin'." The Cornish man stared hard at David, sizing him up and most likely taking in his disheveled state. The other men here couldn't be much better off, David reckoned. The Irishman, who told David to call him Finn, had given David directions to the boardinghouse on Howard Street where Myghal was staying with many of the other Cornish miners. David desperately hoped that Myghal would prove to be a friend—he was in need of one just now.

"Finn told me to ask you about a place to stay."

"Finn sent ye, huh?" Myghal turned to his companions, who were also hanging out on the porch of the boardinghouse. "Finn wouldn't send just anyone off the street. He 'n I 'ave been friends for a long time." He eyed David again, crossing his stick arms over his thin chest. "What can I do fer ya?"

"I just need a place to stay among friends. An affordable place would be preferable."

Myghal grinned broadly. His dirty, reddish hair seemed to glow in the light coming from the street lamps, and he appeared skinnier than one of the planks on the porch. "We might just be friends. And this place is more than affordable. Right, fellas?" Appreciative laughter rang out in the brisk night air.

70

Tossing his head back a bit, Myghal said, "Ye can call me Michael, if ya'd prefer."

David wanted to smile at the confused accent, which sounded like a mixture of English, Irish or Scottish, and American West. He managed to keep a straight face and acknowledged the recognized challenge.

"I'd prefer to call you Myghal, if that's all right."

"Hear that, boys?" Myghal guffawed loudly, sending his thin frame into spasms. "He likes m' God-given name." He straightened and offered his hand. "Well, then, I'll be askin' fer yer name, and then ye ought to step on in and git some sleep."

David clasped the man's bony hand and gave it a good shake, pleased. "My name's David."

Myghal pulled David up the single wooden step and put an arm around his shoulders. "C'mon in, David. Reckon ye can join us here men from Cornwall, iffen ya'd like."

The acceptance felt good. As he walked into the boardinghouse, though, David thought that sleep might feel even better.

"Jacob isn't here yet?" Elizabeth wasn't sure what to think as she walked into her brother's house—without her brother in it. Annabelle fiddled with her hair, now in a blond braid, and shook her head.

"I'm sure he'll be here soon," Joe reassured her, his tone dark.

Silence filled up the parlor until its originally expansive feel became stifling. Annabelle finally asked, "May I get either of you anything? I'm sure all of your walking has made you thirsty."

Elizabeth cringed at the reminder of her small rebellion.

"I think some water fer both of us would be good." Joe turned to Elizabeth and asked, "How'd that be?"

"Fine." Meeting Annabelle's somber gaze, she offered a timid smile and added, "Thank you."

Nodding, Annabelle walked out of the room. This time, Joe didn't let the silence come back.

"How 'bout I show ya the ranch this weekend?"

Elizabeth collapsed into a chair and considered his request. It felt so good to relax, and she slumped farther into the cushions. Maybe she could find some rest from all of her emotions at Joe's ranch. Well, his brother's ranch.

The mere word "brother" upset her, so she dismissed that thought quickly.

"I think I'd like that."

Joe gave her a bright smile, possibly even brighter than the chandeliers above them that had been lit while she was out. She couldn't help but smile back.

Her smile quickly vanished when the door opened to reveal a man she had never met but recognized with some blossoming part of her heart.

This was not what a happy reunion between brother and sister should have looked like. Joe ached to witness the uncertainty on Jacob's face, but what hurt him more was the thought that Jacob didn't even deserve this—the opportunity to meet his sister and intrude on her respectable and untainted life. Swallowing hard, Joe didn't even bother to try to relax his stiff shoulders or unclench his tight fists.

"Jacob." Elizabeth's word came out on a breath, only noticeable because of the complete silence in the room. Her hand shook as she brought it to her face, cradling her cheek as if she were comforting herself, shielding her gaze from her good-for-nothing brother. But Elizabeth couldn't know who Jacob really was. And Joe hoped it would remain that way.

"Elizabeth." Jacob smiled awkwardly, but his eyes lit with a hope Joe recognized as genuine.

Elizabeth finally closed the gap, shuffling slowly at first, and then rushing to Jacob as he stood still in the doorway. Her embrace seemed to shock him, and the wide smile on her face that appeared as she pulled back to look at him was beautiful. *Beautiful...*

Turning away, Joe studied the wall covered with a bright wallpaper that couldn't completely hide the barrenness behind it, which showed up in the corners where the paper was peeling.

This is wrong. What good could Elizabeth gain by making the journey to this evil town? Joe suddenly wished he had told Elizabeth a lie. That her brother had left years ago. That no one would know where he now lived.

If only doing her that kindness wouldn't send her away from him, too.

His fist slammed into the arm of the chair he was sitting in. A curse slithered from his mouth, and Joe was sure he himself was more surprised than Elizabeth or Jacob, who jerked toward him. The horrified expression on Elizabeth's face drove him out of the chair.

"I apologize, ma'am," Joe offered as he practically shoved Jacob aside to get to the door. "I best be goin' now. I'll be by in a few days to escort ya to the ranch." There was nothing else to say.

"You don't have to go." Elizabeth's voice was quiet, uncertain.

Joe paused at the door, then yanked it open. "Yes, I think I do."

She wouldn't understand, but he had no strength of will left to remain there. He rushed out of Jacob's house, away from Elizabeth's confusion, and out into the night air. The sounds of saloon music sickened him, and he headed down the street toward his boardinghouse, where he could sleep for a while. At least, he hoped he would sleep. But sleep would probably elude him, just as everything else he really wanted in life seemed to do.

Chapter 10

BLACK PERMEATED THE SKY, but Elizabeth couldn't find solace in the darkness behind her own closed eyes. Two days had passed since they'd arrived, and she had to see David, to tell him about meeting her brother and to make sure he had found a place to stay. Why hadn't he come to see her yet? Worry churned inside her as she slipped from under the covers and donned her dress, the one David had bought for her in Cheyenne. If he wouldn't come find her, she would go find him.

Quickly brushing her hair and braiding it, she slipped out the bedroom door and headed for the front of the house. Annabelle had gone to bed long ago, and Elizabeth had heard Jacob leave, so she wasn't too afraid of being caught. Taking a deep, confident breath, she opened the front door and left the house.

Now, where to go? She was completely uncertain as to where she would find David. Her only thought was to search in town and see if anyone had met him yet. Elizabeth clutched her skirt as she made her way down the steep hillside. The wind blew steadily, practically pushing her off the path that sloped its way to C Street. It was rather desolate with the night spreading across the dotted brown hillsides around Virginia City, nothing like the flat peacefulness of her farm or the solid strength of the Rockies. Her sigh was lost, snatched away by the river of air, and as she approached the center of town, saloon music flowed toward her. A shiver of apprehension trailed down her spine, and she hoped that someone would know where David might be.

Stepping onto C Street, she followed the music and noted

that the saloons were rather crowded. She headed down the street toward the Delta, wondering briefly if she was being too foolhardy. But surely saloons were gathering places for all sorts of folks, not just the dangerous ones.

She walked past some rude, staring men outside the open door and went inside. It was somewhat dim with smoke, but still the brightness and the noise took her by surprise. Long green felt-covered tables and round wooden tables—with cards and patrons scattered atop and around them—covered half of the room. Elizabeth averted her eyes, heading instead for the bar, where several men were gathered drinking some form of alcohol. She wasn't so naïve as to think that clear-looking liquid was water.

"Excuse me," Elizabeth began, tapping the arm of one of the patrons at the bar. The man turned and smiled at her, but the gap-toothed grin was rather unnerving. "Do you know David…?" Elizabeth paused, panicked that she couldn't remember if David had ever mentioned his last name.

The man laughed loudly and set his glass down hard, not seeming to care that the liquid sloshed onto the counter. "I've known quite a few fellas named David, ma'am. Any one of them in particular ya care to know about?"

Elizabeth huffed at him, which only made him and the man standing next to him laugh. "Yes. I…can't seem to recall his last name, but he's new in town and last I heard he was looking for a job."

"I'm sure he's not the only one," the man said as he elbowed his friend. They shared another laugh over that, some joke she didn't understand.

Anger rose up inside her, and she barely resisted jabbing her finger at the unkind man. "Surely there must be someone here who has met him," she managed between clenched teeth.

"Best of luck to ya, ma'am." With that, the irritating man turned back to his drink. Strangely, she felt grateful not to be the focus of his attention anymore.

Spinning around, she didn't try to hide her frustration. The smoke in the room, combined with the bright lights and the realization that she had no way to find David, made her eyes water, and a tear slipped down her cheek before she could stop it. A gentle hand touched her shoulder before she could wipe the tear away.

"Are ye all right, lass?"

Elizabeth turned and met the gaze of a tall, red-headed man, who looked nice, if perhaps a bit impish. Trusting that his mischievousness didn't outweigh the kindness in his light brown eyes, she took a chance and said, "Well, no, not really. You see, I'm lookin' for a young man named David. He—"

"David, did ya say? Is this man new to town?"

"Yes!" Elizabeth rubbed her eyes and smiled, feeling like perhaps she had done the right thing.

"And might ya be his gal?" His smile was wide, and she didn't know how to respond. Would this man treat her better if she already belonged to another man?

"I…ummm…well…"

Before she could offer a more intelligible response, the man called across the crowded room to someone seated at one of the gambling tables. "David, yer gal's here!"

A few chortles followed along with the man's booming echo, although the general din of the room didn't diminish in its wake. Thankfully, no one seemed to notice Elizabeth's flushed face, nor her surprise at seeing David jump to his feet at the sound of his name. His eyes quickly searched the room and froze when they landed on her. She couldn't tell if the heat she felt came from embarrassment or anger. Both of the feelings bled together into a red that melted over her cheeks.

Well, she wasn't going to stand around waiting for him to come and make his excuses. She turned and weaved through the men who blessedly paid her little mind as their eyes remained riveted to those cursed felt-covered tables. Hurt and confusion filled her, and she wished she was brave enough to push all of these men more thoroughly out of her way. As it was, she had to squeeze past them, and the sense of being insignificant and annoying was acute.

When she finally made it out the open doors, she stepped onto C Street and stormed away—not back to where she had come from, but toward the outer edge of town. Maybe she would walk all the way down into the canyon and beg Joe's family to let her stay early. A bitter laugh escaped her mouth, knowing she had nowhere to run from her thoughts, and afraid someone wouldn't stop her, leaving her alone.

But not defenseless. No, the tension rising inside her would be enough to spew venom at anyone who dared to try and come near her. She would be far less kind than a rattlesnake. And there wouldn't be time for anyone to hear her warning.

"Elizabeth!"

She didn't turn around. Just continued stomping down the street, wanting to yell at the wind for daring to cool her. Now wasn't the time to let her anger lose steam.

A hand touched her arm, but no scream left her lips. She knew that gentle touch, could sense his pleading before she even whipped around to meet his troubled gaze.

"What were you doin' in there?" Her question was a biting one, and Elizabeth didn't quite understand why she cared so much.

"I was only playing a few card games with some of my new friends. Can't fault a man for that." He sounded like a little boy trying to appease his mother. The wind started to tug the rage from her grasp, and Elizabeth hated the feeling.

"A few 'innocent' card games can lead to much more that is far from innocent—you know that." As much as she wanted the sarcasm to scald him, she found it barely warm enough to fight the sympathetic chill in the air.

David smiled. "Elizabeth, we just arrived here. I'm only getting to know the men that I'm living and working with." She bit her lip as he hurried to add, "If it bothers you so much, I'll stay away. I suppose I can play cards just as easily in the boardinghouse as I can in the Delta."

A gust penetrated her long-sleeved dress, and all the fire inside died. She shivered. "I didn't mean to sound like your mother." When he flinched, she reached out and touched his shoulder. "It's not my place. I was just so shocked to find you there, although I had hoped someone there would know where you were."

"You were looking for me?" He took off his coat and held it out. As he helped her into it, she was reminded of the night he'd put his shirt on her after the incident with the bear, his hands lingering on the buttons...

He drew her close as he waited for an answer. She placed a hand on the spot on her side where she knew the discolored bruise remained, only barely. Then she nodded against his chest.

"I told you I would come back, didn't I? I told you I would let you know where I was." He led her up another street perpendicular to C Street, back up toward Jacob's house.

"I know. It's just that I had so much to tell you, and I was worried when you didn't come back right away. It's been a couple of days, you know."

He squeezed her shoulders. "I'm sorry. It's just been a long couple of days. I found work at one of the mines and a place to stay with some Cornish men."

"Like the red-haired man at the Delta?"

"Myghal." A smile was evident in his voice. "He's an interesting one, but he's a good man. Don't judge him too harshly for having some fun at our expense."

"You sound like you know him pretty well already."

"Well, I suppose it's a bit soon to know what he's really like, but I think he's a trustworthy fellow. I guess we'll know for sure later on."

Elizabeth liked how he included her, made it sound as if they were both going to stay for a long time.

"So what had you all eager to see me?"

They stopped to catch their breath, although Elizabeth supposed it was mostly for her sake, David being a mountain man and all. She looked up at him, silhouetted against the night sky, his hair and eyes looking so dark, yet so familiar. There was that light smile on his face as he stood close, head bent down a little as if the smallest threat was all that it would take for him to draw her back to his side and protect her, shield her.

In that moment, she forgot to tell him about her worries regarding Jacob, how odd she felt, certain that something was amiss even though she was thrilled to finally meet him. She forgot to tell him about her upcoming trip to Joe's ranch, about her concern for Annabelle's happiness, or even about her need to send word of her arrival to Sarah Anne.

As she stood there, huddled near him, she remembered instead the nights they sat by the fire, that first evening he'd rushed into the river to save her, the moment she glanced up to catch him watching her as she marveled at the field of wildflowers. So she reached up and softly kissed his cheek.

He turned toward her then, briefly meeting her gaze before touching his lips to hers. She wrapped her arms around his neck and met his kiss, eager to return it. The connection was sweet, secure, and she hardly noticed when he reached down and lifted her up into his arms, deepening the kiss and holding her close. The wind continued to blow around them, embracing them, cold and wonderful as it contrasted with the gentle heat of that moment.

When David pulled back, his eyes were closed. Elizabeth let her head rest against his shoulder, a smile never fading as he carried her the remaining distance to her brother's house. She didn't protest being in his strong arms, and not once did he protest the effort of the remaining uphill climb. There were no words, just wind and warmth.

Chapter 11

"YA READY?" Joe smiled wide, pleased to see Elizabeth and Annabelle standing outside the house, Elizabeth clutching a small bag tightly to her chest. They both appeared quiet but happy, and Joe thought again how nice it was that Annabelle now had someone to talk to. Elizabeth yawned slightly, trying to cover her open mouth with one gloved hand.

"Tired already? We haven't even started down the mountain." Joe relished the smile and blush that appeared on Elizabeth's face.

"I'm sorry. There's just been so much to adjust to lately."

Joe paused, pulling back his hand from where he had reached out to help Elizabeth with her things. "Would ya prefer we wait till another time?" He genuinely cared, but he still held his breath, afraid his hopes for this visit back to the ranch would all be dashed.

A little laugh from Elizabeth brought his breath back in a rush.

"No, of course not. I've been looking forward to seeing your home. It won't take too terribly long to get down into the canyon, right?"

"Well, not too terribly long, no." He winked at her, and she laughed again as she handed her bag to him. While he secured the bag to the back of one of the horse's saddles, he saw Elizabeth hug Annabelle out of the corner of his eye. Annabelle's expression of surprise softened to one of pleasure.

"Ya sure you and Jacob don't mind me being gone for a

couple of days?" Elizabeth sounded concerned.

"Don't worry. You just have a good, safe trip."

"And you're sure you don't mind…?"

"I will send your telegram to your mother this very morning." Annabelle smiled and shooed Elizabeth off the porch. "You make me feel like *I'm* a mother. You don't need my permission to go anywhere, you know." But Annabelle didn't seem frustrated one bit. Joe grinned.

"I'll see you soon!" Elizabeth called back, and then she turned to Joe, squinting in the bright morning light. "Which horse am I riding?"

"You can ride the paint."

Elizabeth gasped as she took in the horse's appearance. Was it just the light, or were her eyes watering? She walked over to the black and white horse, reaching out to pat its neck. "What's its name?" Her question wobbled, and he felt his mouth tighten in concern.

"Her name's Mary."

She glanced up at him, head cocked, the sheen evaporating from her eyes when the warm hint of a smile appeared.

Joe gave her a tilted smile in return. "She was my brother's first love, before he married Naomi. Now Mary's mine, along with this here bay, Copper."

"Men pick such interesting names for their horses." Elizabeth shook her head, pulling herself up onto Mary's saddle before Joe could help her.

"Oh?" Joe mounted Copper and led them down the street.

Elizabeth didn't elaborate, but she gave him a secretive smile when he looked back.

"Guess that's all the information I'll be gettin' then." Joe didn't mind. It was enough that Elizabeth was teasing him, and he was taking her back home with him for this visit. The sun coaxed an even bigger smile from him as they left Virginia City behind.

The sunshine flowing down the hills and pooling in the canyon below made Elizabeth giddy. There was just something about sunlight that made an ordinary visit seem like an adventure. Although this wasn't really an ordinary visit. She hardly knew Joe, and she hardly knew what to expect in this canyon of his, but she couldn't deny a little tremor of excitement that was causing her hands to tremble.

"It's all downhill from here."

Joe's voice flew on the wings of a slight breeze, back to where she sat on Mary. She glimpsed the downward path Joe was headed toward, her eyes widening.

"That looks rather steep. Are ya sure it's safe?" Elizabeth wasn't sure if the shaking in her hands came from excitement or fear.

"I've traveled down this path hundreds of times. You'll be fine. Jest follow me."

The trail dropped sharply down the canyon wall, eventually turning right once the path met with the canyon floor. "Oh, dear."

Thankful that Joe was ahead of her and couldn't hear her or see the trepidation on her face, she allowed Mary to follow Copper down. At least the trail was familiar to the two horses.

She debated within herself as to whether she dare look into the canyon. Yes, it might make her even more frightened, but she reasoned that she'd rather face a little fear now than be completely in the dark as to what she could expect once she got down there.

So she glanced to her right. And another gasp escaped her lips.

The scattered tents, animals, and people were not what she had expected at all. She spied a ranch house set back a piece from the hubbub, but who on earth were those other people? Joe had failed to mention anything about them to her.

Anger and confusion replaced the fear she had felt moments before. The only boy she had ever really spent much time with before leaving Golden was Amos. She had imagined her own brother would be just like him, and her brother's friends would be good, trustworthy men. But as she stared at the foreign scene below, she realized anew that Virginia City was far removed from her farmhouse, and this man she was following might not be safe, no matter how Jacob and Annabelle felt about him. She had been foolish to blindly follow this man who hadn't prepared her for the truth of the canyon—whatever that truth was.

"Joe?"

"Yes?" She saw him turn his head to the side, waiting to hear what she had to say. Well, she wouldn't disappoint him.

"Who are they?"

"What?" Genuine uncertainty filled his voice.

"You know who I'm talking about. You failed to mention how crowded the canyon is."

"Oh. Well…I didn't tell ya?"

"No."

She waited for his answer. As seconds turned into minutes, she wondered what she was doing with a relative stranger, headed toward some place far different than what she had pictured. How did she know she could trust him?

"I want to go back, Joe." Even as she said the words, she knew it was much too late. They were already near the canyon floor, and there was nowhere to hide among the bush-like piñon pines and sagebrush.

Joe reined in Copper and turned to face her.

85

Joe realized that his lack of complete honesty had been the wrong move. He regretted the man he had become in Elizabeth's eyes.

"I'm so sorry I didn't tell ya. I didn't know how to really explain this, and I was afraid you might not want to come if I told ya."

She tilted her head, watching him with what appeared to be a combination of curiosity and wariness as she leaned farther back in the saddle. He better proceed cautiously.

"Ya see, me and my family are obviously not the only ones livin' in the canyon. It's sort of, well, a place where the unwanted people of Virginia City are forced to come."

Elizabeth's eyebrows scrunched tight over her bright green eyes. "I don't understand what you're sayin'."

"I'm sayin' that Virginia City may be filled with some un-savory sorts, but a lot of folks there see themselves as better than others. They go to St. Mary's, or the Presbyterian church, and they think that they have a right to look down on people who are different." Joe realized that his voice was getting heated, so he took a deep breath and added, more calmly, "There's a Jewish community that's been forced to come down here. And some outlaws have settled here, as well, but we don't generally tolerate them as much. It's just a mixed group of people unwelcome in town, so we let them stay here. We don't own all of the canyon, so it's not like we could force them completely out anyway."

Elizabeth turned to take in the canyon's inhabitants. "So they live like nomads down here?"

He could see the compassion in her eyes, and he blew out a breath. Her rigid posture still spoke to him of the likelihood of her fleeing, but there was hope.

"Purty much. We all get along all right, as long as they leave our horses alone."

Her eyes scanned the groups of people and finally settled on the ranch house, back toward the other side of the canyon.

"As ya can see, it's a different sort of situation. I didn't know how to tell ya about it. I'm sorry, Elizabeth. Please give me another chance? My family would love to meet you."

"I don't know."

"I'll watch out for you. You'll be safe. I promise."

She bit her lower lip and gripped Mary's reins tighter. "I suppose, since I came this far…"

Joe smiled wide and reached for her horse's reins. "I'll lead ya to the ranch."

His smile faded when Elizabeth didn't return the gesture. He had a long way to go to make up the ground he lost. He never backed away from a challenge, though.

Chapter 12

THE BEAUTY OF THE NIGHT could really have been enhanced by some peace and quiet. As it was, Elizabeth felt a headache coming on, and she had a difficult time thinking over the events of the day. Didn't all these people living on the canyon floor realize that the day was over?

"Can't think with all the noise?"

The deep voice startled her, causing her to jump up from her seat on the porch steps. Joe's older brother, Seth, stepped out from the shadows by the door, his face lit slightly by the glow of his pipe. He studied the sky. "You get used to it after a while. It all sort of fades into the background." He glanced at her. "You might even find you like it."

"Do you?" Elizabeth asked, curious.

"Yeah." He drew long on his pipe and blew the smoke up to the stars. "You know what I like most?"

She shook her head and waited, arms crossed over her chest to ward off the chill.

"The fiddle. Some of those folks play the fiddle like they have no cares. No ranch to run. No herds of horses to protect from the mountain lions. No worries."

"Maybe not the same worries."

Seth regarded her silently, the smoke continuing to rise above him and flow through the canyon with the wind.

She cleared her throat. "The music might be more of an escape than an expression of joy. I'm sure that if they're really outcasts, some might feel unwanted. And some have probably come out west only to have their dreams of fortune crushed."

He stared straight ahead, and she wondered what he was thinking. Perhaps this man didn't want to hear what she thought.

"How did Joe find you?" His distant gaze never wavered, but she was surprised at the abrupt change in topics.

"Well, I came to Virginia City looking for my brother. Joe found me at the train station and told me where I could find him."

"Who's your brother?"

"Jacob Lawson. He runs the—"

"Yeah, I know him." His dark eyebrows lowered, and she sensed disgust in his tone.

"What is it? What do you know?" Eagerness and dread mingled in her voice.

He glanced at her again. He took the pipe out of his mouth and seemed about to reply when the front door opened.

"Elizabeth?" It was Joe.

Seth tipped his head and walked back into the house.

"Is everything all right?"

Elizabeth would have found Joe's concern sweet if not for the frustration flooding through her, as deep as this strange canyon. "I'm fine."

"Couldn't sleep?" He edged closer to where she remained rooted on the stairs.

She nodded and sat back down with a huff.

He sat beside her on the steps. "I guess I've become used ta the noise. And you have to admit, all those fires in the camps do look sort of purty."

She snorted. "Do you know somethin' about my brother that I should know?"

A prickly pause. Then, "No."

She glanced over at him, skeptical. His blond hair glowed

in the light of the fires, the moon, and the stars.

He smiled gently. "Everything's fine. Yer brother just works harder than many people in Virginia City. There's no shame in that." He looked away at that last line, grinding out the words as if he didn't believe them.

She stood and hugged herself against the cold. The wind and the stars were beautiful, but their loveliness combined with the echoing sounds of the camps was more haunting than enchanting.

Joe rose to his feet beside her, and she turned to him. "It was great to meet your brother and his wife. I guess I'm a bit worn out after all. Good night."

"Good night." His whisper followed after her as she walked across the porch to the house.

Before she closed the door, she glanced back one last time. He stood with shoulders hunched and a hand covering his eyes.

"How're the mines treatin' ya, me friend?" Myghal smiled knowingly as he leaned on the outer wall of the boardinghouse, showered in afternoon light. David couldn't hide a grimace. A man wasn't made to work in those conditions. David had never thought that beneath the cold earth he had slept on many a night, there was a heat that would make him feel like he was being melted from the inside out. And the explosions he set off with a stick of dynamite and a cry of "Fire in the hole!" seemed to shake the foundation of the world.

"Probably no better than they're treating you," he finally replied, smirking as Myghal laughed loudly over that. He had to admit, Myghal's exuberance put him at ease. There was a sense of welcome among the Cornish that agreed with him.

Myghal leaned in conspiratorially. "And how be your girl treatin' ya?"

David had no ready answer. A few nights ago, their kiss had sent his spirits rising higher than they'd ever been. Yet, when he'd tried to see her two days later, Annabelle informed him that Elizabeth had gone to the canyon with that Joe fellow to visit his home.

"Ah, I see. Which is it? Ye've found another girl, or she's found another man?" Myghal's eyes were more sympathetic and somber than David had ever seen them.

"There is this other fellow who keeps following her around. He took her to visit his home for the past few days."

Myghal shook his head and pushed off from the wall. "Ye were askin' for this, ya know. Listen here, David. Ye've been leavin' her alone too long. I know ye've got yer work in the mine, but ya need to go see her at least once every day, even if yer tired. Ya gotta stake yer claim, me friend."

They started walking down the dirt street, and David pushed his hands into his pockets. He wasn't sure if it was the hot sun or nervousness that caused sweat to gather on his forehead. "It's not like I haven't wanted to see her. Just the other day I went to the home where she's staying with her brother and his wife, only to find she was gone on that little trip. What was I supposed to do? Track her down and bring her back?"

"Is she back now?" Myghal bumped David's shoulder with his own.

"I don't know."

"Well, go find out, man! Yer not being aggressive enough. That other fellow's goin' to waltz right in and steal yer girl. Believe me, I know. If ye don't step in soon, yer goin' to lose her."

David stared at Myghal, wondering what sort of heartache was hidden beneath his jovial exterior. He didn't sound bitter, only resigned.

"All right then. What do you suggest?"

"I thought ye'd never ask." Myghal smiled again and headed over to another boardinghouse down the street. "That girl of yers seems awfully sweet on ya. She came to a saloon to search for ya, for goodness' sake. Time for ye to show her some sweetness, too."

David ran a hand through his hair, which seemed to be permanently darker due to the coal dust from the mine. "What are you talking about?"

Myghal walked over to a bush planted by the boardinghouse, covered in yellow flowers. "Yer in luck, me friend. The Cornish roses are in bloom in the heat of summer." A look of pride crossed his face as he gazed down at the pastel flowers bathed in a soft butter color. "A group of us brought some seeds to plant where'er we settled in America. These little beauties remind us of our homeland."

He picked one and handed it to David. "Take a few of these to yer lady. I guarantee her heart will be yours forever."

Taking the small, delicate flower in his work-callused hand, David smiled in gratitude. These blooms weren't blue like the sky, but they were yellow like the sunlight. It was a perfect gesture.

"Isn't that David?" Annabelle asked as she rocked back and forth in the rocking chair on the porch.

Elizabeth squinted in the morning sunlight, surprised and pleased to see David walking toward the house. "That's him!" She felt her face grow warm, although she blamed it on the sunlight slanting toward them.

A soft smile lit Annabelle's features as she continued to sew one of Jacob's shirts.

Standing, Elizabeth placed a hand over her eyes and waved with the other hand until she saw David wave back.

"He looks like a man with a purpose on his mind," Annabelle observed, watching David's approach. "Did I tell you that he came to visit while you were away?"

"No." Elizabeth shook her head, a slight frown replacing her wide smile. She glanced back at Annabelle. "What did he say?"

"He just asked if you were here. He didn't stay long. Although he did seem rather disappointed to discover you were gone." Annabelle looked up with wide, innocent eyes, but the upturned corners of her mouth gave her away.

Elizabeth blushed again and turned back around to find David standing at the bottom of the steps.

"Good morning." His smile was bright, and she returned it.

Noticing he was holding something behind his back, she felt her eyebrows rise as she asked, mischief saturating her tone, "What are you hidin'?"

A beautiful bouquet of little wild roses appeared. She gasped with delight. "Oh, David! Where did you find such lovely flowers out here in the desert?"

"You remember Myghal?"

"Yes?" Her eyebrows fell in uncertainty.

"Well, his countrymen brought the seeds here all the way from Cornwall."

"They're just lovely." She clutched them close and looked down at them admiringly.

"I'm glad you like them." Pleasure warmed his voice. It sent a thrill of joy through her to know that he wanted to make her happy.

"I love them! Annabelle...?" Turning to where Annabelle observed the scene from farther back on the porch, she saw that her sister-in-law anticipated the question.

"There should be a pitcher or vase somewhere in the cupboards. Might I see them before you bring them inside?"

Elizabeth handed the bouquet to Annabelle, touched by the look of child-like enchantment on her face. Some blond wisps fell forward as she bent over the bouquet, and Elizabeth marveled at the woman's beauty. She reached a hand to her own hair, wondering how she appeared to others. To David. Shaking the self-centered thought away, she offered a smile when Annabelle handed the flowers back to her.

"They are absolutely wonderful."

Elizabeth agreed. Rushing into the house, she found a vase and pumped some water into it. As she filled it, she considered— not for the first time—how Virginia City got such clear, delicious water so far away from a proper water source. Jacob had told her about the flume, how the water came from a lake above the grand Lake Tahoe. And something about a reverse siphon underground, which she sort of understood. The pressure from the incoming water pushed the rest of the water down and then up to where it was needed. The stories he told her about people he knew riding logs down the flume years ago were incredible. What a wild, curious place this was.

Once she had enough water in the vase, she set the roses in it, placed it on the table, and headed back out to David. He stood talking with Annabelle, but he stopped when he noticed she had returned. His smile made her think about the kiss they had shared, and shivers of awe swept through her.

"I was thinkin' maybe we could take a walk, if you'd like." If he only knew her thoughts, there'd be no hesitation in his offer.

"I'd love to." Would she ever be able to stop smiling when she was around David?

"Have a good time," Annabelle said as the two of them stepped down from the porch. Elizabeth waved to her and then set off beside David.

They weren't far from the house before David asked, "Why didn't ya tell me about the trip to the canyon?"

Her smile twisted into a grimace. "I was going to tell you. When I found you at the saloon, in fact. But I got…distracted. There was a lot I wanted to tell you, but it didn't seem that important when we…ya know…"

David's face turned red, and she placed a hand on his arm. "I didn't mind. Being distracted, I mean." Then, realizing she had been too bold, she quickly let go of his arm and stopped talking. Now she was certain her own face blossomed red, as well.

"I'm glad." He grinned playfully. "I suppose I didn't mind, either. You being distracted, I mean."

"David!" She was mortified at where the conversation had gone. Was it possible to be mortified and happy at the same time? His laughter only served to warm her heart more.

As they stepped down onto C Street, though, she instantly sobered. "Can I ask you to do something for me?"

She sensed his eyes on her, studying her.

"Of course." His words were certain, but his tone was hesitant. "Just don't ask me to be friends with Joe." When she turned a horrified gaze toward him, he chuckled. "I was just teasing."

Taking a deep breath, she pointed to her brother's store. "I don't know what it could be, but there's something I don't know about my brother. Something important. Joe won't tell me. His brother didn't get the chance to tell me. And Annabelle would never say anything. Will you please find out for me? He's my brother. I can't stand to have this secret between us."

David put a hand to her back as they navigated the crowded wooden sidewalk. After a while, he finally asked, "Are ya sure you want to know whatever it is your brother is hiding? Maybe there's a good reason no one is willing to tell you. Maybe…" He took a deep breath and finished, "Maybe you should leave it alone."

"He's my brother! I know it's something bad. I'm not that naïve. But I want to know. Please, won't ya help me?"

Pausing outside Jacob's store, they both looked in, to where Jacob was assisting several customers. "I don't know, Liz."

"Please." Her whisper was a plea as she met his gaze.

A moment passed, and as she waited, she saw the compassion grow in his eyes. She knew before he gave his final answer that he had resolved to help her.

"All right. I'll see what I can find out."

"Thank you." She smiled up at him and tucked her arm in his as they entered the store.

Chapter 13

NIGHT PRESSED DOWN on the hillside as Elizabeth sat on the steps of her brother's porch. The sun was setting behind her. As it touched the tip of Sun Mountain, scattered clouds of red crept across her peripheral vision, sparks of fire fanning across the sky. The approaching darkness, less bold but far more consuming, sent a shudder down her spine.

Movement caught her eye just then, and she let out a gasp. "Joe, ya startled me!"

His gentle smile put her at ease, though, as he came and sat down next to her, clasping his hands around his knees. "Sorry. I guess ya didn't see me comin'."

She returned her gaze to the clouds. "No. I was distracted by the sky. Isn't it strange tonight?"

He looked up at the lingering pink and shrugged. "Yeah."

The following silence ate at her like the darkness. She wanted to ask him about her brother, wanted to pry out the knowledge he held so tightly in his grasp, far above her reach, like Amos holding something above his head when he was in a mood to tease her about her shortness. She wished she could forget about it, but whatever the problem was, it made her feel that her new friends and family were out of her reach, as well. She couldn't ignore that.

Still, no words came as she turned to Joe. She knew he wouldn't betray her brother. Or maybe he was trying to shield her. But she didn't want to be barred from the truth. Didn't he know that?

"What is it, Elizabeth?" He studied her, wary.

She huffed out a sigh and looked down at her feet, bound tightly in her boots as they rested on the lower step. Shaking her head, she said nothing.

"Are ya homesick?"

Perhaps in some ways she was, but she shook her head back and forth again. Homesickness was not her primary concern at the moment.

"I'm glad."

Genuine warmth filled his voice, and she startled when he cupped her cheek with his strong hand and turned her face to his. Without hesitation, he pressed his lips to hers.

"I appreciate you coming with me." David offered Myghal a tight smile as he walked down the slope toward Elizabeth's brother's home. His nerves were on edge, from more than just seeing his girl.

My girl. His smile turned true, and he pushed aside the uncertainty. He was just concerned the late visit might be taken the wrong way. "I only want to stop and say goodnight to Elizabeth, maybe let her know that I'm keeping my word."

Myghal grinned as he ambled alongside David. "I see yer takin' my advice. Ne'er let a day go by without seein' her face, that's me motto."

David nodded, anticipation churning in his gut. They turned toward Jacob and Annabelle's house as the stars slowly appeared, the moon nowhere in sight. As they approached, he noticed the silhouettes of two people on the porch.

Suddenly Myghal grabbed his arm.

"Perhaps we better pay 'er a visit tomorrow, my friend. Didn't ya say there was a lot ye needed to do tonight?"

David made no reply. The sound of his own breathing and slowed heartbeat drowned out the other noises. His fists clenched at his sides, and in a flash his heart sped back to life. A red haze covered his vision, brighter than any remnants of the sunset.

Instead of running the rest of the way to the porch and pounding that no-good Joe into a bloody heap, as he wished to do, he spun around and headed farther down the mountainside. His little Liz had made her choice then.

"Where are ya goin'?"

The nimble Cornish man caught up with him, but David had nothing to say.

"C'mon, David. What's say we go back to the boardin' house?"

David shrugged off the hand Myghal placed on his arm. "I have a promise to keep. I told her I would find out what her dad-blamed brother was up to, and I aim to do just that."

"Perhaps another day? Ya didn't tell her *when* ye would find out."

David halted and stared into his friend's worried gaze. "I'm not going back to sit and stew over this in the boardinghouse, all right? I've got to do something, and I might as well be doing this. If you're not going to help me, then just leave me alone."

"Maybe this is a big misunderstandin'. Ya don't want to be doin' somethin' ye'll later regret." The wiry man spoke calmly, soothingly. His boyish face appeared much older tonight, with more lines around his light brown eyes that held an ancient knowing. "I know what trouble can be gotten into when yer hurtin' o'er a woman…"

David's heart twisted painfully, making him wonder if perhaps he did need to calm down and not charge headlong into disaster.

The thought flitted through his head in a moment's time,

the trail of its wings overtaken by that blood-red haze. He needed to *do* something. The last thing he wanted was to be alone with his thoughts. So he strode purposefully down to C Street, leaving his friend behind. He didn't bother to glance back, knowing that Myghal stood where he left him, looking on helplessly.

That thought didn't deter him from his mission, though. He patted the holster at his hip, making certain the revolver he had bought days ago was right by his side. Who knew what he would encounter this evening? Beyond the loss of his green-eyed forget-me-not...

Hot anger fueled David as he barged through the door of Jacob's business. The man had to be somewhere close by, as Jacob supposedly worked all hours of the day and night. Darkness met David's eyes, except for a glow coming from the back of the store.

He made his way slowly toward the faint light, every thought focused on finding the brother that had led Elizabeth to this hellish place. He could take his rage out on the man after he discovered whatever awful secret he was hiding.

An empty back room with only a cot in the corner and several boxes of supplies met his scouring gaze. But it was the door on the other side of the room, standing slightly ajar, which caught his attention. Opening it the rest of the way, he walked into a very short hallway lit by kerosene lamps, with several rooms off of it and a stairwell going down to a lower level.

Going down to D Street. *Sporting Row.*

He took a deep breath, finally putting the pieces together in his mind. Jacob's store on C Street was the same building that housed a brothel on D Street. Only a town built on a hillside could manage something like that. He was certain Jacob owned both businesses. Flashes of the wealth evident in Jacob's home ran through his mind—the fancy parlor, the chandelier, the blue cushions, the red carpeting. And with two businesses such as these, it was no wonder he was gone both day and night.

David stomped down the stairs. "Jacob! Come out here. I've got somethin' to say to you."

Jacob materialized from a room on the lower level, counting some bills in his hand. "Quit your shouting. You'll disturb the other customers. I've got one open room, so show me the cash and I'll show you in." He glanced up then, and recognition flooded his eyes. Greenish-brown eyes, if the lamplight didn't lie. A color not so different from Elizabeth's. "Do I know you?"

"You should. I'm Elizabeth's…" He hesitated. The emotion from moments before rushed over him, and he choked out, "Friend. I escorted her here because she was so desperate to leave her safe, decent home to come out and meet her brother. A brothel owner. Does Annabelle know about yer night job?"

Instead of the rage David expected his accusation to elicit, something like guilt shone in Jacob's eyes. He somehow kept it hidden from his voice as he asked, "What do ya want?"

"Elizabeth sent me here, to find out what you've been hiding from her." He glared at the man, watched him squirm under the scrutiny.

"Well, I guess you know now. Anything else I can do for you?" Jacob turned away, resignation and forced nonchalance mixing in his words. He slid behind the counter and filled a couple of glasses with what looked to be whiskey. "Have a drink."

David stormed over to the man. "Don't ya realize how this news will devastate Elizabeth? Your innocent little sister came to this godforsaken place to meet *you*."

Jacob faced David from behind the bar, his gaze hard, steely. The look punched David in the gut. *Too much like Elizabeth's eyes…*

"I've done some things I'm not proud of. Haven't we all? I'm providing for my wife the best way that I can. We could never live a normal life anyway." Jacob gulped down a shot of the vile liquid.

David eyed the other glass cautiously. There was a sudden, strange urge inside him to wash down the craziness of the night with a shot of whiskey. Maybe it would help him forget. Before he could question himself, he downed the glass and set it down hard on the counter. "What do ya mean, you could never live a 'normal life'?"

Jacob shook his head, his dark brown hair falling across his eyes. "Everyone in this town knows anyway, so you might as well know. Annabelle? She used to work here before I married her."

David's face reddened, and he downed another glass of whiskey that had somehow become full again while he was listening.

"No one respects her. So I give her the best life I can." Jacob paused a moment, gaze vacant, before adding, "I love her." Running a hand through his hair, he lifted his head and stung David with his stare. "I'll not risk losing my money again. We'll never be poor, if I can help it. She'll never come back to this life, and I'm her only assurance of that."

He cursed and continued pouring whiskey. David had no idea how many shots he drank while he listened to Jacob.

A soft hand on his arm startled him. A beautiful young woman with bright blond hair and a painted face gazed up at him, her expression sly, but with something deeper in her creek-clear eyes. He had the sensation he was diving in to rescue someone again...

"Hey, boy. You look like you could use some company tonight." Her red dress was shocking, hitched up above her knees and cut far too low in the front. David tried to look away, but he found himself mesmerized, his gaze dipping beneath the waves of lace. Everything seemed hazy, and he couldn't remember if he was dreaming or where he was.

"I know what it's like to be cast aside. But we can make each other feel wanted tonight." Her smile drew him, and he found himself smiling back.

"I'd...like...that," he agreed, concentrating hard on his words.

"Mind if I take him away, Jacob?" She looked to Jacob with a pout and begging blue eyes. Her lips were so red.

Jacob never looked up from the bottle in front of him. "Whatever you want, Sally."

David followed Sally, not really sure where he was going. Her figure covered in that gorgeous dress beckoned him onward. She was the rope he had to cling to, Liberty waiting for him on the shore... All he could think about was how much he didn't want to be alone.

She led him to a room at the back of the first floor. He could hardly take his eyes off the girl, but he did notice that there was a faded carpet by a big bed, as well as a pitcher and basin in a corner by the door. The one window was covered tightly with curtains. The light blue color of the few furnishings calmed him, reminding him of Sally's eyes. The spaciousness of the room felt freeing.

"Come here." Sally led him by the hand, across the carpet, to that big bed. She sat him next to her and started to unbutton his shirt. The motion of her hands absorbed his attention. She was helping him, like he had helped Elizabeth into his shirt to warm her.

His fingers shook, and even though Sally had only undone half of the buttons, he drew her hands around his chest and kissed her hard. She giggled as he lowered his head, pressing his lips to the hollow of her neck.

He was lost, adrift, but he ignored the urge to claw to the surface, to breathe the air of reality. He rather liked the feeling of drowning…

Very real water suddenly splashed over him. He jumped to his feet, shaking the hair out of his face. Shock coursed through him as he took in Myghal standing by the bed, holding the now-empty pitcher of water in his hands, stubborn determination etched into the lines of his face.

"Hey! What do you think yer doin', mister?" Sally's voice was filled with incredulity.

"I'm sorry, lass, but this man isn't supposed to be here. He already has a woman." Myghal never took his eyes off David as he said the words. "Come on." He put his arm around David and led him out past Sally's sunken form on the edge of the bed, past Jacob sitting in a chair in the front room with the empty bottle of whiskey, and out the door into the cool night air. David gulped it in as if he had broken the surface of a raging river. Then he doubled over and wept bitterly.

Concern slithered through Elizabeth as she paced in front of the boardinghouse where David had claimed he was staying. She had seen him, noted his hurt and anger as he witnessed Joe kissing her. But by the time she had found the presence of mind to push Joe away and call out to David, he was already heading down the hill toward town. Where did he go after he saw her and Joe? Why wasn't he back yet?

She had left Joe sitting on the porch steps. She had no idea what he was thinking either, and she hadn't had the heart to look at him after she had pushed him away, breaking off the kiss. Opting to face David's raging emotions instead, she had decided to go straight to the boardinghouse and await his return there. She had never expected him to be gone so long. Other men had brushed past her, but she paid no attention to them, and thankfully no one bothered her. Maybe she had already been identified as David's girl. That thought brought a small smile to her lips, and she hoped that David would give her a chance to explain what had happened tonight.

Leaning back against the front wall, she looked up at the stars, wishing she could weave those distant jewels into her hair and sew them onto her dress. She wanted to be beautiful. *For David.*

The sound of shuffling jolted her out of her thoughts, and she glanced up to find David and his friend, Myghal, heading toward her. She waved, and they stopped. She got the distinct impression that Myghal wanted to run in the other direction. She couldn't make out what he said, but David stayed back and Myghal approached her alone.

"Lass, I think it'd be best if ya go home tonight and come back in the mornin'." He looked sad, as if someone had passed away.

Her heart beat hard and fast as she peered past his thin frame to David, who was standing in the middle of the street, staring up at the stars. After a moment, his eyes met hers, but the darkness kept her from reading the look he gave her. He began to walk toward her, but Myghal blocked the way. In a low voice over his shoulder, he repeated, "Please go home, lass."

"What's goin' on?" Elizabeth ducked past Myghal and went to David. "If this is about the kiss, I can explain. I never…"

"Yesss," David interrupted. "I sssaw ya kissin' that viper."

She backed away a couple of steps, horrified. "Why, David, you're drunk!" The stench of his breath followed her as she retreated.

"What did ya expect"—he took a gulp of the desert air—

"me to do? You had a kisssso I thought I should, too."

Cold dread whipped through her. "What do ya mean?" When he resumed his search of the stars, unresponsive, she voiced the question she wasn't sure she wanted answered. "What did you do?"

Finally, he looked back down at her, and there was a sorrow in his eyes that seemed to be at war with the callousness. "I f-found yer brother." He staggered a little, and Elizabeth reached out to steady him, but he shoved her away. "Don't touch me! You shouldn't...shouldn't touch me." Then he began to cry.

Elizabeth froze, rooted to the street, her heart breaking. She looked to Myghal, but he just watched, as if he had seen all this before and was helpless to do anything about it. "David?" Hesitantly, she reached out her hand and brushed his sleeve, conflicting desires to discover the truth and to flee tangling inside her.

He looked up then, stricken. "I kissssssed her," he slurred, bowing his head as he spoke. "If Myghal wasn't there..."

"I don't understand."

Clarity filled his eyes for a moment, like a needle poked through a thin canteen. "Yer brother owns a...a brothel. Where Annabelle used ta work. And I f-found him. And one of his girls found me."

Her heart thudded to a halt. What was he saying? About her brother? About himself?

"No." She shook her head and drew her arm back, clutching both hands to her chest. "It isn't true. No!"

Before she could run, David grabbed her arm. "Please, Liz. I didn't mean to. It was only a kisss." His shadowed eyes pleaded with her, but she turned away. His dear, brown eyes—she had never seen them so filled with pain. But something had changed. She didn't know who this man was. She didn't know if she could trust him.

Shaking her head, tears blurred the winking lights above into unfamiliar shapes, strangers. She fled from him, sure that such aching would break her heart into fragments more numerous than those once-lovely stars.

Chapter 14

SHAME. Not even the moment he'd realized no one was ever coming for him after the accident in his childhood had brought about such stabbing shame. While the rest of the boardinghouse seemed to be preparing for the day, and the activity of the town below continued on unimpeded, David just lay there on his cot, feeling sicker at heart than in his mercilessly churning gut. The previous night could have been almost a blur except for the look of fear on his sweet Liz's face. He remembered with absolute clarity her shimmering green eyes, the uncertainty flowing from them as she turned away.

He moaned and turned onto his side. How could so much go so wrong in just one night?

"Don't worry. Yer belly will settle down eventually."

David looked up to find Myghal leaning against the door-jamb, watching him with a mixed look of pity and disgust. David moaned again. He was one wrong movement away from retching.

"Do ye wanna talk?"

"No. I don't even want to think, but I can't seem to stop doing that."

A specter of a smile appeared on Myghal's face. "Well, ye best be gettin' up soon, 'cause ya know ye can't go back and change what happened."

With that, Myghal straightened and walked out of the room, his red hair bright in the sunshine filtering through the grimy window.

Sitting up slowly, David glanced around the bare room. Everyone else was up and getting ready for work, if they weren't at the mines already. He considered Myghal's words and knew he couldn't go back in Elizabeth's eyes or even Myghal's. He couldn't go back to work and just pretend like he still belonged in this terrible town. But, perhaps...

Yes. Maybe he could go back home.

Rising from the bed, he went to the window and looked through the dirty glass at the busy people below. Part of him longed to return to his cabin and imagine that nothing had ever happened. But he knew he couldn't. He pictured himself stumbling around in the silence, seeing Elizabeth everywhere, haunted and miserable. No, he had to go back home, to the family that forgot him. Perhaps he could go back far enough to escape this horrid present and find a way to make peace with his past. It was the only hope for a future he could think of.

Clutching his pounding head with one hand, he rushed out of the room and palmed the front door with the other hand. "Myghal."

The man hadn't gone far, and he turned at David's call. He waited in the street.

David joined him, trying to disguise his belch with a cough. "I've got to leave. It's time I returned home."

Myghal tilted his head, considering him. His brown brows slanted as he asked, "Are ya sure ye know what yer doin'?"

"I'm certain. I can't stay here. You know that." The sunlight fell all around them, as if God were showering him with warmth to bolster him for the hard journey ahead. He bowed his head and rubbed his neck. It was bold of him to think that God would bless him after what he did. An ache pressed against his chest, even as a familiar peace eased the pain. A train trip was exactly what he needed. He would have time alone to pray, to seek God. Something David had been neglecting for far too long.

"Ya know she'll hate ye for leavin' without saying farewell." Myghal stared up at Sun Mountain's peak, his jaw clenched tight. He must have sensed David's urgency, his desire to leave as quickly as possible.

"I know, but I'll hate myself if I stay or try to speak with her now. Maybe it's for the best."

Myghal swung his gaze back to David then, just as the piercing call of the train several streets below reached their ears. "I know."

"Will you watch out for her, though? Just to make sure she's safe."

"I will." Myghal grasped his hand firmly. "I'll miss havin' to try and keep ya out of trouble." The man grinned, the boyish, mischievous look he had worn when David first met him returning for a moment.

"I'll miss you, too." With one last squeeze of Myghal's hand, he turned to gather his things. He was going home.

An odd sense of dread washed over Elizabeth as she awoke to late-morning sunshine streaming through the window. She had locked herself in her room last night, only returning to her brother's home because she didn't know where else to go. Now she pushed back the blanket and slipped on her dress. Urgency pulsed through her, and she couldn't get out of the house quick enough to suit her.

She splashed water on her face, ran a brush through her hair, and then gathered the few things she could claim as hers before silently unlocking the door. The sun's clear light made the house look innocent, clean, but Elizabeth knew better. Nothing seemed safe anymore, especially not her brother's home.

Making her way outside, she paused on the porch. Where could she go?

She sank to the steps, but jumped to her feet a few minutes later when she spotted Myghal. He was heading back up the mountain, probably from some errand in town. Perhaps he would know where she could stay.

"Myghal!" She left the porch and walked purposefully toward him. Surely he could help her.

Elizabeth almost turned around and ran back when she saw the somber wariness in his eyes. "Yes, lass?"

"I was wondering… Perhaps ya might show me…" She fidgeted. There was no mistaking the sorrow on his face. Was he as sad as she was over David's behavior, his revelations? But this was a different kind of sadness, she was sure. Permanent. "Whatever is the matter?"

He sighed and stuffed his hands in his pockets, his tattered shirt flapping like a flag of surrender in the breeze. "You would find out sooner or later. Guess it might as well be sooner." He stared straight into her eyes and declared, "David's gone."

No words came. She was sure the confusion was evident in her eyes, for he clarified, "David left just a bit ago on the V&T. I don't think he'll be comin' back."

The blood drained from her face, leaving behind only a cold paleness. "What do you mean? He…he can't be gone. He wouldn't do that. He wouldn't leave me." The anger and hurt from last night was nothing compared to this. They could have worked it out, surely. Eventually. But he had abandoned her, another blow and another betrayal to her heart.

"When did he leave? Maybe he's still there. Maybe the train hasn't left yet." Frantic, she dropped her bag and ran as fast as she could to the train station. She was afraid her legs would get tangled in her dress and cause her to tumble all the way down the mountain, but still she ran. Panic pushed her on, until she stood at the station, breathing hard, with no train in sight. She heard Myghal calling her name, but she had no answer for him.

When he finally caught up to her, he set her bag down and gently touched her shoulder. "He knew he was doin' the right thing. He needed to go home. Ya both need yer time apart."

"But how could he abandon me? How could he leave me here with no one to turn to?" Tears misted her eyes, and she started to shake, despite the hot summer weather. "I can't trust my brother or his wife. I can't trust Joe."

"David told me to watch out fer ye. You can come back with me to the boardin'house until we get all this settled."

She turned to look at him then, her emotions uncontainable. "He's really gone. What if…what if he forgets me?"

Her pain seemed to be echoed in his eyes. "Ah, lass."

She fell against him then and sobbed into his worn shirt. His thin arms held her close, and his voice broke as he assured her, "I promise ye, he'll never be able to forget you."

Part III:

Remember Thou Me

"According to thy mercy remember thou me for thy goodness' sake, O Lord."

Chapter 15

JOE APPROACHED THE DOOR SLOWLY, afraid that if he came in too quickly Elizabeth would flit away like a butterfly and evade him, as she had been doing for the past two weeks. He leaned his shoulder against the doorjamb and watched her as she sat staring out the window of the boardinghouse. She looked so gentle, so unsure. *So beautiful.*

Elizabeth startled, her gaze flying to his as she became aware of his presence. Her fresh green eyes widened, and she jumped up from the edge of the bed. "Why are you here?"

Taking only a few, painstakingly hesitant steps, he came fully inside the room. "I wanted to see how you were doin'. And I wanted to apologize for offendin' ya the last time we saw each other."

He couldn't apologize for the act itself, though. He had never meant to frighten her, but if he could, he would kiss her as many times as she would let him. No more rushing, though, because what he really wanted was for her to kiss him back. To fall as deeply in love with him as he was with her.

She clutched her hands together, silent for a moment. Then she asked, "How did ya know where I was?"

"Jacob told me."

She flinched at the mention of her brother's name. So she knew. It surprised him that David would have told her, after all that Jacob told him had happened, but his heart filled with sweet relief. No more secrets. Nothing to hide.

A soft smile crept across his face. "You do see why I

couldn't tell ya? I thought I was protectin' you."

She didn't respond, her gaze turned away from him. Taking another step forward, he longed to start again, to begin their acquaintance anew.

Before he could reach out to her, a hard voice intruded. "What are ye doin' here?"

Joe turned to find a wiry man with red hair leaning on the doorjamb where he had just been, watching him calmly with cold eyes.

"It's all right, Myghal." Elizabeth visibly relaxed at the man's arrival. "This is Joe."

Joe had a funny feeling that the man already knew who he was and didn't approve of him.

"What do ya want here, Joe?" Myghal addressed him with a frown.

How could he explain? This man appeared completely unsympathetic, and Joe didn't know how he could explain his need to see Elizabeth—to set things right, to find hope for a future with her.

"Well…?" Myghal pushed off the doorjamb and drew close to Elizabeth, muscular albeit thin arms crossed over his chest.

"He came to apologize and to check on me." Elizabeth bit her lip, her gaze riveted to the floor. He guessed that she was still uncertain about him but didn't like the tension between him and Myghal.

"I wanted to see how she was farin'." He also wanted to ask her to come and stay at the ranch, but he realized that it was too soon for such a suggestion. She wasn't ready for that big of a change, and he doubted that she would trust him enough to come with him yet. He'd just have to keep going slow until she grew comfortable in his presence again.

"Well, ye've seen her now and ye can go."

Myghal stood tall next to Elizabeth, glaring to add emphasis to his verdict. As much as Joe disliked the treatment, he realized that he probably wouldn't respond any differently if he were Myghal. Too much had happened recently, and he had a sick feeling that the kiss he had stolen had been a bigger cause in this mess than he had originally wanted to believe. He knew David had seen them when Elizabeth had pushed him away and called the man's name. And he knew that David had laid claim to her heart before he had ever met her.

Shaking his head, he attempted to dislodge the thoughts. He had prayed for forgiveness, as much as he knew he didn't deserve it. And now was the time for a new beginning.

"Mebbe I can come again sometime?" He directed his question to Elizabeth.

Both men looked to her, and after a moment she glanced up and met his gaze. "Maybe."

There was no guarantee in her words, but he smiled anyway and took the hope she offered. The lovely butterfly's wings were folded tightly together for now, but perhaps in time she would open them again and follow him home.

Several days had passed since Joe's visit, and Elizabeth didn't think she could stay in the boardinghouse a moment longer. She needed fresh air, and as much as she appreciated Myghal's kindness in letting her stay and providing her with her own cot, which he had probably had to pay extra for, the confining space was making her feel ill. She was ready to get away from the small, dusty room.

Myghal was working at the mines today, so she splashed some water on her face, brushed and braided her hair, and headed outside. She didn't really want to walk through the heart of the noisy town, but she didn't know where else to go. Keeping her head down, she forced herself to take one step and then another. The hem of her dress dragged along in the dirt, but she didn't care. The whole dress was in need of a good scrubbing. Maybe she should search for a laundress while she was in town.

But how could she go on like this? Living in a town with nothing but horrible memories?

That's not entirely true. Thoughts of Annabelle's kindness, meeting Joe's family, and the kiss she shared with David filled her mind. Thinking of any kiss was too painful, though, and with that idea the rest of the happy thoughts flitted away, leaving her heartsick.

Oh, God, please show me where to go. I'm so lost. I don't know what to do. She felt a tear slide down her cheek, but she didn't bother to rub it away.

And then he was there. She lifted her gaze to find him watching her, waiting for her in front of her brother's store, the complete compassion on his face drawing her like a moth to a light. No matter what had happened before, she needed him now.

As if he knew of her aversion to her brother's place of business, he left it and walked toward her.

"Joe." He couldn't possibly hear her whisper over the pounding of the stamp mills and the buzz of conversations on the street. Still, he smiled gently and reached out a hand to her. She hesitated for a moment, then placed her hand in his. As she studied his hand, remembering the hands that had saved her from Clear Creek, a sob escaped her lips.

He led her to his horse that was tied up outside the store, the wood of the structure glowing near-red in the daylight. He lifted her into the saddle, then swung up behind her and guided Copper out of town, in the direction of the canyon and his ranch. When they passed the cemetery, she couldn't hold back her emotions any longer. Her whole body shook with confusion and grief.

Joe wrapped his arm around her, letting her lean against him. For a moment, he didn't speak except to call "whoa" to the horse, reining the creature in along the side of the dirt street. He just held her, letting her cry.

"I'm so sorry, Elizabeth," he eventually said. "I never meant to hurt ya or deceive ya."

She gazed out across the deep blue sky and the unending rolling hills, covered with nothing but scattered sagebrush and small pines, all made blurry by her tears. The scene was so desolate, but something stirred in her as she felt Joe's arms tighten comfortingly around her.

"I want to be here for ya, whatever you need from me. Yer not alone out here." He touched a hand to her shoulder, causing her to glance back at him. "I'm grateful to that man, Myghal, for giving ya shelter. Between him and me, you won't be alone."

"I know." Her voice broke.

He wiped a tear from her cheek. "I was thinkin' maybe I could take ya to see Lake Tahoe sometime. It's a bit of a distance, but it would make fer a good place to get away from town for a while. We could ask my brother and his wife to come, too."

She paused for a mere breath. "That would be nice." She met his smile with a small one of her own. The wind sent his sand-colored hair flying toward her, and his Stetson looked like it could be dislodged at any moment. His tender expression and boyish charm were so endearing. "Thank you." She didn't know how to explain her gratitude for his understanding. He seemed to know just what she had needed—to get away from watchful eyes and busy streets.

"Yer welcome. Ya ready to go back?"

"Yes, I think so." The reminder of hope was enough.

The sun hadn't yet risen when Elizabeth awoke one morning a week later. Today was the day they would start their short trip to Lake Tahoe. Initial excitement mingled with a bit of uncertainty, but excitement ultimately emerged victorious. She was weary of staying indoors, mending clothes for the other boarders and reading what few books they had. She practically skipped across the room to the makeshift dressing corner, partitioned off from the rest of the room by a faded curtain.

After getting dressed and packing what little she had back into her bag, she aimed for the open door.

"Are ye sure ya really want to go?"

Elizabeth whirled around, a hand to her heart. Myghal sat on the edge of his cot, running a hand through his hair, looking tired and very worn-out. She must have been too consumed with her tasks to notice when he had entered. His light brown eyes met hers, and she felt the uncertainty rise to overtake the excitement she had felt.

She walked over to the cot and sat down beside him. "Do ya think it's wrong if I go?" She clasped the sack in her lap and looked down, waiting. Pale rays of light forced their way through the dirt-stained window.

She felt a gentle hand on her arm and glanced up. Myghal's jaw worked. "Myghal? What is it?"

"Ye remind me o' someone."

She hadn't been expecting that. "I do?"

"Back in Cornwall, I had me a gal. She was the most beautiful fiery-haired lass you'd ever see. And I thought fer sure we would be married."

He stood, running his hand through his hair again as he made his way to the window. He was silent, his expression troubled.

"What happened to her?" Elizabeth remained on the cot, waiting and watching him.

"I thought she loved me."

His gaze was so solemn, his mouth down-turned like he had just heard some horrible news that would change his life forever. Perhaps he was reliving such a time.

"Didn't she?"

Not taking his eyes from the clouded view out the window, he replied, "I'll ne'er know. I ne'er got the chance to ask her. But I thought we had an understandin'. And then she married someone else."

"Oh, Myghal..."

"I lived it up fer a while after that, but I only felt worse-off, like I was provin' that I ne'er deserved her. So when some other Cornish fellas—friends o' mine—said they was goin' to America to work the mines in the West, I joined them. Thought I'd start o'er."

His gaze finally swung back to her. He appeared so lost, so unsure. Standing, she reached out and touched his arm. He placed his hand over hers. "How could I 'ave been so wrong? I really thought she loved me."

She swallowed, then bit her lip. "Perhaps she did. Maybe her parents told her she had to marry this other man, and she felt that she had no choice."

A soft smile added to his boyish look. "It doesn't matter now, though, does it?"

"But you still love her."

"I'll ne'er forget her. I can't."

"Should we ever forget those we've loved? Maybe our paths will never cross with them again, but can't we still be grateful for the depth they added to our lives?" She shrugged. "Surely God allowed us to love them for a reason. Right?" The last word came out as a plea.

Myghal embraced her. "Perhaps so." Stepping back, he added, "But I hate to see David go through what I went through. Do ye still love him?"

Tears burned her eyes. "He left. Maybe he needed to start over, too."

"His situation and mine are much different, lass. He loves you, and neither one of you is claimed by another—yet."

"But that doesn't mean we weren't supposed to go our separate ways."

He said nothing, but she desperately wanted him to reply, to contradict her and tell her that David would come back for her.

A knock on the door broke the moment. "Elizabeth? Are ya ready?"

"It's Joe." She grabbed her sack and walked to the door. Before she opened it, she turned and gave Myghal a tiny smile. "Goodbye."

He nodded once in her direction, wordless and unmoving. In the ghostly morning glow she thought she saw a tear catch the light on his freckled cheek.

Chapter 16

DAVID HAD BEEN FORGOTTEN, abandoned, all those years ago, so what was he hoping for when he came back home? The train was bringing him closer and closer to the people he had never wanted to see again. He knew it was the right thing to do, but he still felt like that young boy who had turned his back on the family that had turned their backs on him.

David couldn't decide if the miles passed slowly or much too fast. He couldn't tell the familiar apart from the unfamiliar as various landscapes passed by his window. All he knew was that he had made a decision that might have cost him all his dreams for the future. But he could never have planted a healthy future without preparing the land—taking care of the damages of the past.

The farming life came back to him in a rush: memories of spring planting, hopeful summer afternoons, and the season of harvest. What little boy wouldn't have enjoyed that life, the carefree Colorado days with fields and rivers, valleys and mountains all around? *And Elizabeth, making life fun.*

He shook his head, turning his thoughts to his cabin back in Colorado. He recalled sunrises over gray peaks, the satisfaction of hunting for his own food, the briskness of the fresh air through the aspens, and the cold beauty of a night sky full of stars. The life of a mountain man had suited him just fine. *Until Elizabeth…*

The moment he had saved Elizabeth, his life shifted forever.

Settling back into the cushions of the train seat, he continued to ponder the journey he was making. How was his family? Would they be glad to see him, or upset? Would they feel remorseful, or would they even care that he had come back?

Elizabeth's sweet green eyes came to mind again, and he sat forward, the seat creaking in agitation. He wanted so desperately to go back, to find her and kiss her and tell her he would never leave her. But he had boarded the train knowing full well the consequences. There was no turning back.

The scenery continued to wash over his window, and time blurred like the reds and yellows of the passing trees. Fall was coming. His parents would be getting ready for harvest. Perhaps he could help, if they wanted him to.

Why should he even consider helping the ones who never bothered to find him?

He ran a hand through his hair and gripped a handful of strands. *Oh, God, I don't know what the future holds. I don't even know the past all that well.*

Like those trees holding tight to their once-green leaves, he was going to have to let go soon. He just didn't know if he could trust that spring would come again if he loosened his hold.

Chapter 17

HOW IS IT POSSIBLE *to care so much for two men at the same time?* Elizabeth leaned forward in the saddle and ran a hand over Mary's mane as the horse plodded along toward Lake Tahoe. The horse inevitably brought to mind David's Liberty, which he had sacrificed for her. Had she ever properly thanked him for selling his horse, paying their way to Virginia City and taking such good care of her? Whatever she'd told him certainly hadn't been enough. Not enough to express her gratitude. Not enough to keep him with her.

Her heart twinged with an undeniable tug from across the miles, wherever David happened to be, but the distance also pushed her closer to Joe, a man who was helping her heart to heal from the discovery of her brother's terrible secret.

"How ya holdin' up?"

Elizabeth peered ahead at Joe, who had turned slightly in his saddle, genuine warmth and concern in his eyes.

"I'm doing fine. You seem to forget that I traveled quite a way by horseback to get to the train station in Cheyenne." She said it with a smile, hoping the subtle reminder of David wouldn't cause tension between them.

"I do recall somethin' 'bout that." He winked and turned ahead again.

Joe led the way on Copper, Elizabeth following behind on Mary, and Naomi and Seth rounding out the party behind her. Comfort blanketed her with the knowledge that Joe's brother and sister-in-law were coming with them to the lake. She could imagine herself a part of this family, taking trips together and running the ranch in the canyon…

As they continued on their way, after over a day of travel, the scenery subtly changed. Instead of only sagebrush and endless dusty brown, tall ponderosa pines rose around them and the occasional meadow carpeted the ground they trod. Even though the grass was far from green, any new variation of brown was a welcome relief.

The rocking motion of the horse's gait lulled Elizabeth. She pondered the previous night, how they had built a campfire and shared some food and conversation around its flames. It was hard to be lonely surrounded by such kind people, especially with Joe making her laugh with humorous ranch stories. Still, the night out in the wilderness brought to mind nights across the fire from David. Snuggled up in her bedroll, she couldn't help but think of him. Part of her longed to be on the train with him, returning to Colorado and escaping from the mess she had foolishly rushed into here in the desert.

But then she had awoken to find Joe frying ham over the fire, his blond hair looking so soft in the sunlight, tousled from sleep. He had met her gaze and smiled at her, a smile so gentle and bright that she thought perhaps he was the reason God allowed her to come to Nevada.

Shaking her head, she tried to rid herself of such thoughts. Now was not the time to be thinking about something so definite, when her future seemed so far from certain.

"Look there." Joe's voice brought her head up, and she strained to see where he pointed. Shading her eyes from the afternoon sun, she caught a glimpse of a rocky shore and a blue more vivid than the Colorado sky.

"Is that the lake?" Her voice quivered with an excitement she couldn't contain. "Why, it's so blue!"

Joe laughed. "Wait till ya see it up close. You ain't ever

seen such clear blue water as Lake Tahoe."

She could believe it. Her eyes met Joe's, and she shared a tender smile with him. She could believe in clear water and—perhaps—a clear, beautiful future.

"Come on, you've gotta see the water up close!" Joe held out his hand and held in his breath, hoping Elizabeth would come with him. He had been eager to have a moment alone with her ever since they had arrived at the lake and set up camp yesterday afternoon. The sun was shining warm upon the water, and Elizabeth's brown hair took on alternately fiery and golden sheens in the light. She squinted up at him, then turned back for a moment, probably reassuring herself that Seth and Naomi were nearby.

He waited. A slow smile came over her face. She tilted her head back, letting the sunlight pour over her. "You're right," she said. "On such a glorious day as this, we have to enjoy the beauty of nature." Her smile turned mischievous as she met his gaze. "But only if you promise not to push me in."

Laughter rumbled forth, a sweet release of nerves. "I promise, I won't push ya in."

His hand closed gently but firmly over hers, and he felt then that a different sort of bond had been formed between them, deeper than friendship. Walking hand in hand from the camp, they headed toward the shore. The rocks here were large and round, perfect for climbing and finding a seat from which to look out over the lake.

Elizabeth slipped once, and he instinctively grasped her waist, steadying her. Her summer-green eyes met his, and he saw gratitude and warmth there. He felt stronger in that moment than he had ever felt before.

"What about here?" He gestured to the rock they stood on, close to the water but high enough above it to keep from getting wet.

She nodded. They sat side by side, gazing at the lake. But the blue couldn't hold his attention for long, as it was Elizabeth's green eyes he wanted to swim in. She was so beautiful…

"Elizabeth?"

She only barely inclined her head in acknowledgement, continuing to stare at the lake.

"Do ya like it here?"

She nodded more enthusiastically. "It's lovely. I never thought I'd see a lake such as this. Makes me long to see the ocean someday. I can't imagine how exotic and wide the ocean must be."

She hadn't understood his question, but he chose to ignore that fact for a moment. "Which ocean?"

Her eyebrows scrunched in thought. "The Pacific."

"And why is that?"

"I'd like to see what it's like farther west."

Trying to bring the conversation back around, he asked, "So ya like the West? Do ya like it here, in Nevada?"

She glanced over at him. "Yes, I suppose. I like it here, at the lake. Your ranch is very nice, too."

Just what he'd been hoping to hear. He smiled wide. "And me, Elizabeth? Do ya mind puttin' up with the likes of me?"

Surprise flickered in her gaze, which now riveted on him. "Well, no. No, I don't mind. You've been very kind to me." A little smile appeared, as if she was unsure whether a smile was warranted then.

Silence took over briefly while Joe debated within himself what he should do. Surely this sweet girl was a gift he could never deserve. But he desired to make her his own, to cherish and love her forever. Elizabeth was all that he had ever wanted in a wife.

"Elizabeth…" Turning fully toward her, he knelt beside her on the wide rock and pulled the ring out of his pocket. "Might ya be willin'…? That is, might ya consider…? Will ya marry me?"

The silver band shone like light playing on water as he waited for her response. She stared at the ring as if mesmerized, her mouth slightly open, begging for his kiss. *Just one word.*

But no words came. She fiddled with her skirt, her eyes turning as glassy as the lake. He knew who had to be on her mind. His chest cinched a little tighter, and he shifted back to take some of the pressure off of his knee. If she just said yes, they could move forward.

Forget about David. I'm here. He's not.

He couldn't bring himself to say the words aloud. "Elizabeth…?"

He had a home for her, a place to take care of her and provide for her and a family. That had to mean something.

She closed her eyes, blew out a breath, and then—finally—met his gaze. "Yes."

Shock and sweet relief poured through him, and she laughed at whatever expression he made.

"I said yes!" Her giggles skimmed across the water. "Aren't you going to kiss me?"

Her smile turned bright, hopeful, and he was sure it mirrored his own. He let out a whoop and sent his hat sailing through the air, out toward the water. Then he bent down and scooped her up into his arms, kissing her with all the exuberance and passion he had ever longed to feel.

When he pulled back, she slipped a little, and he drew her back to his chest again. Her muffled words spoken into his shirt made him chuckle. "Ya best be careful, or we'll both end up in the lake."

"Sorry." He wasn't sorry at all. Grasping her hand, he declared, "Let's go tell my brother and Naomi the good news!"

No more rocks for Joe Clifton. No more boulders lying in his path, obstructing the flow of his life. He was ready to forge ahead like a clear, wild river.

Chapter 18

"GOLDEN! Now arriving in Golden!"

David glanced out the train window, the apprehension that he had expected to feel conspicuously absent. It felt right somehow. He was home.

Grabbing the saddlebags he had brought with him—his only luggage—and placing his hat on his head, he headed to the front of the car. The train came to a stop, screeching a little on the tracks and puffing out an exhausted breath of smoke. David understood. It had been a long journey for him, too.

Memories poured over him as he walked down the steps and onto the wooden platform. He thought of his mother, the smell of baked bread surrounding her like a cloud and the snow-dusting of flour powdering her apron. He recalled following his father and Amos around, trying to help out on the farm as best as a young boy could. Then he thought of a young girl with a smile bright as the sun when he had given her those little blue flowers as they played by the river. An ache stole over him.

There was no need to ask for directions as he walked through town. It was as if he had been through here only a few months ago, buying sugar or flour for his family and rushing home in order to help his ma get food on the table. Ignoring the jeers of early drunken fights and the female shoppers calling out to one another, he skirted horse droppings in the road and headed out of town, to the farmhouse he had once loved so well.

Fields of quietness eventually replaced the town's cacophony.

The gentle music of nature, punctuated by jingling harnesses and enhanced with the smell of hay, greeted him, each step taking him further back in time. Any moment he expected to hear his sisters giggling, or his mother humming out in the garden, or Amos yelling and asking him to go for a swim in the river running through their land.

But no human voices called to him as he caught sight of his family's land. The farmhouse appeared a bit worse for wear, but was still as welcoming as he remembered it to be. A few flowers bloomed in front of the porch, and the sun shone warmly upon the pink blossoms.

He stopped a few yards away, not wanting to break the peacefulness of the scene or the cheerfulness of unmarred and happy memories—memories made before he had fallen into the creek and been lost to his family.

A breeze enveloped him with a feeling of melancholy, bittersweet but tinged with hope. Taking a deep breath, he walked forward, stepped onto the porch, and knocked.

Footsteps sounded, and then his mother opened the door, a smile hovering on her lips as she eyed him warily. He knew he should speak first, but he couldn't utter a word. Years seemed to melt away as he saw the mother he had loved so dearly, but they quickly rushed back up to meet him. He felt the impact of each one as he saw the sorrow on her face, the added lines around her eyes, and nary a look of recognition or acceptance. He shouldn't have come.

"I'm sorry, ma'am—"

He didn't have a chance to finish. A strange look passed over his mother's face, and a shiver coursed through her. Squinting, she stepped forward, then gasped. "Casey? Can it be...?"

His old name sounded so strange, like a childhood nickname long forsaken. "Ma." His vision blurred.

As soon as he spoke the word, his mother's hand flew to her mouth. "My little boy. Oh, my baby boy! My Casey."

He reached out and pulled her to him in an embrace, and she sobbed against his shoulder. He had never known what it was like to be taller than his mother, to pass from the stage of her little boy to her grown son, a son that could take care of his family. Would he ever know how much he had missed?

"Ma?" A young woman appeared at the door, concern tightening her features. Her brown hair was braided down her back, just like it had been all those years ago – except then her braid had been shorter and just right for yanking. He could still hear her cries of outrage as she chased him from the house.

"Louisa."

The girl startled when he spoke her name.

Another young woman appeared in the doorway. She had to be Christy. Even as toddlers, their differences had been obvious. One brunette, the other blonde. One more serious in nature, the other flamboyant.

Christy peeked over her sister's shoulder at David. "Who is it?" Her light hair was pulled up into a fashionable style, and her blue eyes shone with curiosity.

His mother didn't look up as she clung to him, so he replied, "I'm your brother, Casey."

His sisters both gasped and stared as if he had told them he was President Cleveland, come for a visit. He offered them a gentle smile and held out his hand to Louisa, unsure if she would accept the handshake.

Both Louisa and Christy let out a cry and crowded into his embrace. He hugged them all tightly, afraid to let go, afraid to discover that the moment was just a dream. Any lingering anger built up over the years crumbled at the force of their welcome, their emotions high as if he was a war hero or perhaps the prodigal son. Whenever he had let the thought of returning tumble around in his mind, he always pictured the door tightly closed, no one willing to allow the past into a home too small for him.

"I just can't believe you're alive," his mother breathed, shaken. She pulled back and held his face in her cold hands. "You have to know that." Her gaze pleaded with him, her tears now silent as they tracked down her cheeks.

David couldn't respond. Instead, he asked, "Where's Pa?"

And then it hit him, why his mother had appeared so sad before she even knew who he was. Their silence cut him deeply. He had waited too long to come home, and now he would never have the chance to know if his father would have opened the door wide for him, as his mother had.

"He…fell from the hayloft…" Louisa attempted to answer, but the tale was obviously too gruesome and raw to share yet, sending a shudder through his sister.

He let them all go and stepped out of his mother's hold, furiously rubbing at his eyes. He would not let them see their older brother as weak. This was his chance to be the help his family needed, although it was coming years too late.

His mother straightened, heading for the door and rubbing her teary face with her apron. "Come in, Casey. I've got supper cooking. Amos will be in from the fields soon, and we've got so much to talk about."

Like how you stopped looking for me? How you gave up on me? Even though the hot anger was gone, the smoldering hurt remained. Still, he followed the girls inside. As he stepped over the threshold, a kinder warmth spread through his heart. His pride had been beaten low through the years, but now there was no room for pride.

He was home.

Chapter 19

COULD THIS PLACE *ever feel like home?* Elizabeth clung to Joe as they walked through town on their way to Jacob's house, avoiding the drunken brawls echoing from the saloons. Why, it was still the middle of the day, and men were already drunk! She tightened her grip on Joe's arm.

Joe laughed and hugged her arm close to his side. "It's fine, honey. They'll stay in the saloons. Just don't visit those places, and you'll stay out of danger."

She bristled at his words. Did he know about the time she went into the Delta looking for David?

His finger brushed her cheek. "I didn't mean to imply ya would. I was just tryin' to reassure you."

She tried to relax. The shouts and pounding that marched down the streets hadn't bothered her as much before, when she thought she was just visiting Virginia City.

Well, that wasn't completely true. She had never been sure what she was going to do after she saw her brother. All she had known was that David was there, and she didn't want to go anywhere without him…

Tears burned, and her nose wrinkled. How could she be thinking about David when she was engaged to Joe? She simply had to put him out of her mind. He had obviously forgotten all about her. Life would go on, and she would make this land her home if it meant staying with someone who loved her.

"What's the matter?"

From the corner of her eye, she saw Joe looking down at her with concern.

"I…I'm just… I don't know what I'll say to Annabelle."
And that truly did bother her.

"I know it'll be different, but please don't judge her. She
didn't have much of a choice. And Jacob really does love her."

The mention of her brother's name sent shivers spiraling
through her. She hoped that Jacob wouldn't be there at the
house. She couldn't face him yet. As far as she could tell from
his earlier habits, though, she had no reason to worry that he
would actually be with Annabelle.

Her thoughts were all tangled up when it came to her sister-
in-law. She was so sweet, but what could have caused her to
choose such an…occupation? Of course, Elizabeth had never
known what it was to really be in need. Sarah Anne had seen to
her care ever since her parents died. What if Sarah Anne hadn't
taken her in? What if she had been on her own?

Her emotions tied her insides into knots as she climbed her
brother's porch steps with Joe at her side. He knocked on the
door, and they waited.

A minute later, Annabelle opened the door a crack and
peeked out, uncertainty darkening her expression. Without another thought, Elizabeth pushed the door open all the way and
embraced her sister-in-law. "Oh, Annabelle, I've missed you!"

Joe caught the surprise on Annabelle's face a moment before
the tears came. She hugged Elizabeth tightly, and together they
both cried.

He had no idea what had caused Elizabeth to become so
emotional. He supposed the thought of weddings did that to a
woman. And he knew she had been worried about seeing Annabelle again, after what she had learned.

He was proud of her, and her kindness to Annabelle only

made him love her more. Annabelle needed a friend like Elizabeth. He would be sure to bring Elizabeth into town often after they were married.

Finally, Annabelle and Elizabeth pulled apart, and Annabelle ushered him and Elizabeth inside. The two females sat close together on the sofa in the parlor.

"It is so good to see you again," Annabelle said, a warm smile on her face.

"It's good to see you, too." Elizabeth wiped away stray tears and responded with a smile of her own.

Joe let Elizabeth tell her sister-in-law the news of their engagement, knowing that women loved to be the first to share anything with one another. He stood in the doorway of the parlor, watching them with a smile and smoothing his mustache with finger and thumb as he listened to them. He'd have to get another haircut and shave before the wedding…

"When will the wedding be?" Annabelle asked.

"Well, I want to invite my ma, so I'll need some time to get a telegram to her and make sure she can come." Elizabeth turned to Joe, a question in her still wet, green eyes.

"Perhaps we can wait until spring," Joe offered, although he disliked the idea of waiting several months or more until the wedding. It hadn't even started to snow yet, but it would soon. A winter chill had already invaded the air.

Elizabeth gestured for him to come join her, so he sat down beside her on the end of the sofa, taking her hand in his. "I think it would be good to wait," she reiterated. "That way we have more time to…well, to get to know each other. And Sarah Anne will have enough time to schedule the trip. I really want her to be here."

"I know. We'll make sure she arrives before we get hitched." He winked at her, hoping to put her at ease.

Elizabeth continued to chatter with Annabelle about the

wedding, and as she did Joe let his mind wander. He had a feeling Elizabeth wouldn't be comfortable with staying at her brother's house anymore, and having her stay at the boardinghouse with that man, Myghal, was out of the question. But would she be willing to come down to the ranch with him? Seth and Naomi would be there to serve as chaperones and provide some company, but the snow would probably keep them from town for most of the season...

"Where is your mind today, Joe?" Elizabeth poked him in the side, a wobbly smile on her face.

"Did I miss somethin'?"

"Annabelle wants to know if we could join her for supper."

"Of course."

Spring seemed so far away, but he would push that thought aside in favor of enjoying the smile on Elizabeth's face.

Chapter 20

"HELLO, PA."

David stared down at his father's grave, wondering what his pa would say if he were still alive. Would he have warmly accepted his younger son back from the grave like David's mother and siblings had done? Or would he have sent David away again, if for no other reason than that they could no longer relate to one another after all those years apart?

The small wooden cross was a bit weather-beaten after two years of surviving the elements, sheltered only by a couple of aspen trees by the river. David leaned back against one of the trees and crossed his arms over his chest, hearing only the rustle of the breeze through the leaves and the gentle splashing of the river as it meandered across the field. No little blue flowers at this time of year—and no green-eyed girl to give them to.

Heaving a sigh, he slid down the tree to a sitting position on the dead grass. He kept his arms crossed, afraid to completely relax.

"Why didn't you try harder to find me? I waited for you to come for me."

Just like Elizabeth, David had gone to Clear Creek Canyon in a fit of boyish frustration. He was a headstrong eight-year-old, running from his anger toward Amos for something he had done, something David couldn't even remember now. And just like Elizabeth, he had managed to fall into the swift creek. The only difference was that he had hit his head when the current had thrust him against some rocks at the shore. He had awoken

139

drenched, cold clear through, and lost, unable to remember why he was there or where he was supposed to go. After hours of wandering through the ponderosas, he had come across Frank's cabin.

The man with the scruffy beard and gentle soul had taken him in and given him a childhood as a mountain boy. Perhaps he should have been more angry with Frank, who had never tried to find his family for him. But somehow David had been able to forgive the lonely man when he had learned the truth, even though he was unwilling to forgive his own family. Frank was all David had, the only other person he knew for several years, and their bond was not easily rent, especially considering Frank had wanted him for a son when his own family apparently did not.

By the time he remembered where his home was, his life in the quiet, accepting mountains was all he wanted. By the time his honorary father died in a hunting accident, the feeling of abandonment was complete.

But all that time, he had only been a couple of days away from the farm and his former life.

"Why, Pa? I was so close. How could you just give up on me?" No one but God was there to see his angry tears. He had never wanted to grieve—he'd wanted to be brave in his exile, to stand on his own two feet without sorrowing after a family that didn't care. *They might not have cared, but I did.* He couldn't hide the pain any longer.

"Casey?"

His gaze flew up to find his brother walking toward him. He angled his face away, but not before he saw the concern in Amos's eyes. After a moment, Amos joined him on the grass, leaning back on the other side of the tree and brushing the long blond hair out of his face.

"You know we did our best to find you." A question fluttered in the statement, but the words came out with enough certainty to suggest that David could never have thought anything else.

He had no answer for that. He would have liked to believe it, but doubt was a more familiar friend.

Feeling Amos's gaze on him, he finally said, "I suppose so."

"Pa searched for days. We went to town, asked all of our neighbors—we even went to the canyon. We had no way of knowing whether the marks we found were from a wild creature or you. Of course, you were one and the same at times…"

A grin rose of its own will on David's face, but quickly disappeared.

"Did ya…ever miss me?" He ducked his head in embarrassment and plucked at the grass, knowing it was a childish question, feeling like the tag-along little brother he had once been.

Amos bumped his shoulder, waiting until David glanced up and met his somber gaze. "You're my brother. You're a part of our family—always were and always will be, gone or not." He paused. "Did you know that we always kept your chair at the table? Ma never had the heart to take it away."

David cleared his throat, suddenly clogged with emotion. He got to his feet, and Amos followed. They stood in silence by their father's grave, shade and sun alternately sweeping over them in the gentle wind.

"I go by David now."

Amos stuffed his hands in his pockets and glanced at him. "Why David?"

David shrugged as he offered a self-deprecating smile. "I wanted to be 'a man after God's own heart,' like ma once taught us. Even when I couldn't remember my past, there was something about that name and the Psalms that Frank read that stuck with me." He swallowed, his eyes stinging.

Amos nodded.

As they finally turned away from the grave and walked back to the farmhouse, Amos threw an arm over David's shoulders. "Can I call you David?"

Chapter 21

WINTER WAS A LONG, long season. The snow had accumulated in the canyon, and trips up to Virginia City were scarce at best. Elizabeth enjoyed spending time with Joe and his family, but she found herself often gazing out the window at the piled-up snow and wishing for spring.

Thoughts of spring inevitably brought to mind thoughts of home—the planting season for farmers. She missed planting a garden, working out in the fields with Amos when he came around to help, and baking with Sarah Anne. She did her best to hide her tears from Joe, but homesickness consumed her, along with a longing for David she couldn't seem to put away.

She cared for Joe, and she was sure that once they were married they would only grow closer. She appreciated the kindness he showed her, and the winter was bearable only because of reading and talking with Joe, helping Naomi in the kitchen, and thinking about seeing her ma in the spring for the wedding.

Spring did eventually clear away most of the snow and solitude, and with May's arrival Joe promised to take Elizabeth into Virginia City.

"Are ya all ready, honey?"

"I've been ready for months!" Elizabeth couldn't keep from smiling this day. The telegram they'd received from Sarah Anne months ago said she should get to Virginia City the second week of May, and it was finally time to go to town to wait for her. When she arrived, her family and Joe's family would all head out to Lake Tahoe, where Elizabeth insisted they have the wedding. Elizabeth twisted the ring on her finger in nervous anticipation.

"Well, come on then." Joe tossed her a wink and helped her mount Mary before he swung up onto Copper.

As they passed through the tents of Jews and the other canyon inhabitants, Elizabeth called to Joe, who was riding ahead, "You said we could invite Myghal to the wedding, right?"

"Of course."

"And you're sure Annabelle recalls that the wedding is in eleven days...?"

"Yep. I'm sure she does."

"Good." Excitement filled her as they rode up the trail out of the canyon.

They were silent for most of the rest of the trip to town, Elizabeth occupied with thoughts of the wedding and seeing her ma again. But as they approached Virginia City, Joe asked, "Yer invitin' Jacob, too, aren't ya?"

Elizabeth didn't answer. She hadn't seen Jacob since last fall, and, with a sick feeling inside, she realized that she didn't want to see him again.

Joe turned and waited for her to catch up to him, then reached for Mary's reins. "Ya know you can't just never speak to him again. He's yer brother."

"I know," she said, her tone lacking conviction.

"Elizabeth, honey..."

"I don't want to see him."

"Ya know how I feel about what he's done. What he's doin'. But I hate to see ya holdin' onto this bitterness. He really does love Annabelle, and he really does care about you."

"Don't lie, Joe." Her voice came out low, dangerous.

"Listen, if you get to invite Myghal, Annabelle, and Sarah Anne, then I get to invite someone, too."

"That's not fair." Her fingers tightened on the saddle horn, and she was sure her eyes were spitting sparks at him.

144

"It is fair. Jacob is like my brother, and he is your brother. I'm invitin' him if you won't."

Tears welled up in her eyes, and she wrenched Mary's reins out of his hands. Without another word she galloped into town, hating her tears, her anger, and the strange sense of displacement that had seemed to haunt her ever since David left. She could hear Joe gaining on her, but she ignored him. She didn't slow the horse until she reached Annabelle's home—she refused to think of it as Jacob's house.

Joe reined in next to her, but she jumped off Mary and headed straight for the porch. A hard hand gripped her arm, and he spun her around to face him, a look of concern mixed with frustration in his honey-brown eyes.

"Elizabeth, so help me… Ya can't just go gallopin' through town! You could have run someone down or got in front of a stage."

She turned her face away from him. Through her tears, she told him, "Yer jest a big bully. Why won't you leave me alone?"

"Elizabeth…"

"No!"

She tried to wrench out of his grip, but he only grasped her arm tighter and pulled her to him. Pounding his broad chest with her fist, she tried to vent her fury. But the action only brought a flash of memory—hitting David's chest, his anger as he shoved her away, and a realization of unspoken love.

You will not control me!

I've only wanted to help you. To protect you. Don't you understand?

The fight left her, and she fell to her knees, sobbing.

Joe sank down with her and held her close. "Shhh. It'll be all right."

They could have stayed there for a long time if Joe hadn't seen something. She felt him stiffen before he scrambled to his feet. He mouthed only one word, but it sent fear raging through her. "Fire."

Annabelle. Annabelle's in there. Elizabeth stared up at the house, horrified. The flames came from where she knew Annabelle and Jacob's room to be. And it was a dry day.

Joe took off running down C Street.

"Joe!" she screamed. "We have to get Annabelle out of there. Where are you goin'?"

"I've got to get to the fire station. Alert the firefighters," he called back over his shoulder.

His long legs sent him careening down the hillside. Swinging her gaze back to the house, she stared at the growing flames, helpless and terrified. Why hadn't Annabelle come out yet? There was no question she was in there. She hardly ever left the house.

Tearing her gaze away from the glare, she glanced around, hoping to find some other men who had come to help. A few seemed to be gathering water buckets and supplies to help put out the fire, shouting back and forth to one another, but no one was going into the house. Didn't they know someone was still in there?

Oh, God, help her. Help all of us. Please. She ran into the building, hating herself for not going in sooner. Once she began to move, urgency overtook her, and she rushed through all of the rooms, calling out Annabelle's name. When she had run through the parlor and the kitchen and found no one, she took the stairs two at a time and barged into the bedroom. She was nearly knocked back by the heat and the smoke. Her eyes watered as she fell to her knees, staying close to the ground, trying to see where Annabelle was. The beautiful red and gold bed was engulfed in flames, as well as the carpet on the floor and the wallpaper near the bed. Peering through the smoke, she finally saw Annabelle sprawled on the floor by the bed. She bit back a cry and crawled toward her.

The heat burned her cheeks and throat as she approached Annabelle and attempted to shake her awake, hoping she wasn't injured. "Annabelle." The name came out on a whisper that crackled before turning into a cough. "You've got to wake up! We've got to get out of here."

When Annabelle didn't move, Elizabeth pulled her limp body against her side and tried to drag her to the door. She made very little progress, though, and the smoke made it difficult to breathe. Inching her way forward, she prayed, unable to beg more than, *Oh, God, please!*

Suddenly, hands reached down and grabbed Annabelle, carrying her away. Then someone scooped Elizabeth up, as well, and raced down the stairs, out of the house, and into the dusk.

Coughs racked her body, and she clung to her rescuer.

"Elizabeth." The word dripped with agony and admonition. "What were you thinkin'? I could have lost you."

Joe. He held her close, looking down at her, tender worry and regret causing his eyes to squint. His wheat-colored hair stood out in various directions, and part of her longed to reach out and smooth it. Another part didn't want to be anywhere near him.

"Joe," she rasped.

"Shhh. Don't speak. I shouldn't have left you." He rubbed her arms with such force, she winced.

All she wanted was to shut out the images of blinding, twisting light and the sounds of the house crackling and falling apart. Instead, she sat up, hoping to catch a glimpse of Annabelle and the person who had rescued her. Her heart clenched when she saw them.

Her brother cradled Annabelle, weeping. He ran his shaky hand down her long blond hair—turned dark with soot—over and over. The firemen seemed to have the fire under control, but nothing compared to the relief that seared her when she saw Annabelle's eyes open. Jacob kissed her forehead tenderly and guided her head to his shoulder, tears raining down on Annabelle's tangles.

The town wouldn't burn again. Annabelle was alive.

Elizabeth clutched Joe's shirt, wishing she could rejoice in the victories. But her mind was consumed with the memories of flames and Joe fleeing.

Chapter 22

DAVID HAD HOPED to avoid any shopping trips for as long as possible, but Christy and Louisa broke him down with their pleas, determined as they were to buy new fabric to sew dresses for an upcoming barn dance. While the town of Golden had calmed since his childhood, he still wasn't about to let his sisters go there alone.

Also, he had lost the wrestling match with Amos, so he had to be the one to take them.

The whistle of an incoming train called to him through the damp air as he walked with his sisters into the heart of town. Every time he heard the cry, it pained him like a physical blow. He desperately wanted to hop on board and see Elizabeth again. Make sure she was all right. Tell her how much he loved her. But something always stopped him. As much as he wanted to go to Elizabeth, he couldn't leave his family, not after they had finally been reunited again. It was his responsibility to stay, to not miss another moment with them after all the memories they had lost.

He felt a hand holding him back every time the urge to leave hit him. He was waiting for something, felt the truth of it floating in the back of his mind and the depths of his heart. Perhaps God was telling him to wait on His will, as hard as it was and as much as he wanted to take matters into his own hands. Still, inaction made him feel powerless. What kind of man would do nothing when his sweet friend, his forget-me-not love, was living in a mining town with her rascal of a brother and a man who stole kisses from her?

What kind of man would ever leave her there in the first place?

Groaning inwardly, he tried to keep his step light as he escorted his sisters down the wooden walkway and opened the door of the shop for them. He ran a hand through his dusty hair, unable to hold back a smile when Louisa thanked him and Christy elbowed him playfully as she walked past.

He gave them a wave before closing the door after them, choosing to drop onto a beat-up, tobacco-stained wooden bench and wait outside rather than brave the yards of fabric and Christy's excited squeals.

"Casey?"

The tentative female voice brought his gaze up, where a woman around his mother's age stared at him, rooted to the sidewalk.

He jumped to his feet and slid his hat from his head. "Yes."

She gasped and took a step back, her gold and gray hair falling from its confines as she shook her head. "Of course, I heard from your ma months ago that you were alive. It's just such a shock, to see you for myself. You really are alive." Her eyes grew wide, as if he appeared before her as a ghost instead of a flesh-and-blood man.

He gave her a small smile. "Yes, I'm alive, ma'am."

"Oh goodness, you wouldn't remember me, would you? I'm Sarah Anne. Elizabeth's ma."

His smile fell. He bunched up his hat in his hands. "Mrs. Pruitt."

Her blue eyes took him in from head to boots, and her lips lifted. "You've grown into such a nice young man." Clutching a valise closer to her skirt, she added, "I wanted to thank you for watching out for my girl."

His face burned with shame. "I don't deserve your gratitude, ma'am. I should have brought her straight home. It was foolish of me to take her to Virginia City." *More than you could ever know.*

"It's all in the past now. I'm just grateful, so very grateful she made it safely to Virginia City." She sniffed, apparently unable to continue as she lifted a handkerchief to wipe her eyes. Before he could apologize further, she recovered. "I'm on my way there, myself, to attend her wedding."

David's blood froze in his veins, but she didn't seem to notice the way he stiffened.

"I wish she had found someone here, and I can only hope he's a decent boy. Like you." She bestowed a smile on him, but when she caught his expression, her eyebrows scrunched.

Then the train whistle blew again, and she shifted her valise to her other hand. "I really must be going." Her mouth opened again, as if she wanted to add something else, but she ducked her head and turned without another word.

Her wedding.

Elizabeth's getting married.

To Joe.

His mind scrambled frantically, even as his heart seemed incapable of one more beat.

As he took a few steps after the woman, he remembered his sisters and glanced back at the store. He closed his eyes in frustration, then rushed to catch up with Elizabeth's ma, stopping her in the middle of the street. She studied him, and he had the odd sense she knew the things he wasn't willing to tell her.

He licked his dry lips, escorting her the rest of the way across the street as he said, "Please tell Elizabeth…" *What?* He scuffed his boots on the rough wood of the sidewalk, then lifted his pleading gaze to Sarah Anne. "Please tell her I wish her well. Tell her I…" *Love her.* But he couldn't say the words.

Sarah Anne's eyes were pools of compassion. "I'll give her

your message."

She left then, scurrying to the train station.

He stood under the Colorado sun, watching. *Please, God, guide us all.* Even as his body felt tethered to the spot, freedom reached down and pulled him from the rush of emotions as he listened to the voice that whispered, *Wait.*

Chapter 23

THE WIND PICKED UP and the late afternoon sunlight poured down on Joe as he stood next to Elizabeth, waiting for the train that would hopefully bring her ma. The breeze brought no relief to Joe's constricted chest, though—he felt sure his breathing would be permanently labored. Even though he had his arm about Elizabeth's waist as they stood together, he felt like they had grown miles apart since last week's fire.

He had made a mistake, a big one. Perhaps an unforgivable one. When he had seen the smoke rolling from Jacob's house, all he could picture was the devastation left behind from the fire over a decade earlier, when he had been just a boy. Seeing so many buildings burned to the ground and the sorrow brought by the loss, the fire had turned Joe's heart cold.

He couldn't stand the idea of the town burning up again. His first thought had been to run to the fire station, to recruit as many people as possible to help control the fire.

He had forgotten about Annabelle...and for a moment he had forgotten about Elizabeth.

He cringed inwardly, knowing that if he had been thinking clearly and rationally, he could have spared Elizabeth the pain and saved Annabelle himself.

Tightening his hold on Elizabeth's waist, he tried to take in a deep breath. Still, his breathing remained shallow as fear kept a painful grip on his chest. He was afraid. Afraid of what might have happened. Afraid of what could yet happen. Afraid that somehow the fire wasn't the only thing keeping him and Elizabeth apart.

Every time Elizabeth closed her eyes, flames danced across her eyelids. She shuddered, and Joe drew her closer to his side.

Apparently the fire had been caused by a candle, which Annabelle had forgotten to blow out and accidentally knocked over in her sleep, having gone to bed early. It was terrifying to think of how quickly a fire could escalate.

Bits of conversation from the day she had first come to Virginia City, when she had first met Joe and he had told her about her brother, came back to her as she stood waiting for the train.

I think the fire of '75 really struck fear in him, though, ya know? So many people lost everythin'… With a decade separatin' him from that disaster, ya would think he would finally feel secure.

Tears came to her eyes. She hadn't understood then what Joe had meant. Perhaps she could never fully comprehend the horror and fear Jacob had faced all those years ago, but she felt closer to understanding now. Her brother had moved on, but he had been afraid to lose everything again. So he had rebuilt one business and established a new, more lucrative one, so he could be financially secure. And then, over the years, he must have fallen in love with one of his employees.

Owning a brothel was wrong; she knew that. She held onto the hope that Jacob knew that, too. His priorities had to shift in the face of potentially losing what he really held most dear— Annabelle. The good that God had brought out of the evil of her brother's past.

Raising a hand, she wiped a tear from her cheek and shaded her eyes, hoping for a glimpse of the train. Her ma would be here soon, and she would get to introduce her to Jacob and Annabelle.

When the train finally whistled in the distance, Elizabeth realized with a start that she was wishing one more person would be on it. *David.*

A small crowd had gathered at the platform, waiting for the train to come to a stop and for its passengers to step into the daylight. Several minutes crawled by like several hours as Elizabeth waited with her heart in her throat—wondering, hoping.

A few people she didn't recognize stepped down from the train. And then she felt tears gather in her eyes as she saw a man step off and help her ma to the ground. Sarah Anne searched the group of onlookers, and when Elizabeth met her gaze she gave a little cry.

"Ma." The months that had passed since she left home seemed like a mere trip into town, or perhaps her whole lifetime. Time made no difference as she rushed into the arms of her mother.

She sobbed as relief washed over her and her ma's tears fell on her head. "My little girl." The words brushed over her in calming strokes. It was as if no one else was there.

"I'm so sorry, Ma," she managed, her voice halting and broken. "I'm so sorry I ran away." The last word came out in a low wail, and she buried her face in her mother's warm shoulder. She wanted to clarify her apology. To tell her mother she was sorry for not coming home first. For not sending her word sooner. But she couldn't manage any other explanations.

"I know, dear. It's all right. It's all right." Sarah Anne spoke soothingly, running her hand down Elizabeth's hair and holding her tight.

Finally, Elizabeth remembered Joe. Pulling away slowly, she offered a wobbly smile and gestured to the man she was going to marry. "Ma, this is Joe. Joe, this is my mother."

Sarah Anne glanced between the two of them, then stepped to Joe and embraced him. "It's nice to meet you."

Joe smiled as he squeezed Sarah Anne. "It's a pleasure to meet Elizabeth's ma." Then he stepped back, grabbed Sarah Anne's valise, and led the way to the hotel.

Even though Elizabeth knew in her heart that it was hopeless, she couldn't resist one last look behind her at the train. David never came.

Elizabeth had returned to Lake Tahoe thousands of times in her imagination. In her mind's wanderings, there had been sunshine, cheerful birdsong, and wildflowers lining the trail. Now that she was really making the trip, rain followed their group as soon as they left Virginia City on horseback.

The weather did nothing to calm her nerves, and she knew she was shaking from more than the late-spring cold. It wasn't really excitement, either. Uncertainty paralyzed her at the thought of being married, of a permanent partnership.

As her horse plodded along, she refused to dwell on thoughts of David.

Glancing around, she did allow herself a small smile at their wedding party, composed of Joe, his brother Seth, Seth's wife, Sarah Anne, Annabelle, Jacob, and Myghal. Myghal looked about as unsure as she felt. He was, after all, David's friend.

Jacob rode up alongside her, and for the first time since she had found out about his secret, she offered him a smile. His response couldn't quite be called a smile, but his features softened and his green eyes brightened a little.

"Joe has been a good friend of mine for years," he began.

She wound the reins around her hand as she waited.

"He's a good man, and he would make a good husband."

"Would?" Her forehead wrinkled in confusion.

He sighed. "I hardly feel qualified to give you brotherly advice, or to intrude on your affairs. But do you really love him? When you first came here almost a year ago, you were smitten with that young man—David, I believe his name was. The one who brought you here."

"How would you know?" She sensed the venom in her voice and tried to let it drain away. "You were never around," she added quietly.

He sighed again and swiped his gloved hand across his forehead. "I know. And I'm… I regret what I've done."

"I love Joe." Was she saying it for his benefit or hers?

"I know. But this David fellow… He came to find out what I was hiding. He was angry because he knew how much I had hurt you. Elizabeth, that boy loved you. You don't ever get over love like that."

His gaze sought out Annabelle then, and Elizabeth's heart warmed. How much of what he had done had been for his wife's sake?

Thinking about David only hurt her and muddled her emotions, so she asked in a small voice, "What will you do after the wedding?" Jacob hadn't gone back to work since the fire, but Elizabeth was afraid he might eventually return to it.

He set his jaw. "I'm selling the store and closing down the brothel. I have enough money set aside to take Annabelle somewhere else, somewhere where I can spend more time with her and protect her. I've done her wrong by working all the time."

"I think our parents would have been proud of that decision. And how could anyone not love Annabelle?"

He finally smiled as he sat taller in the saddle.

"Perhaps you could come back to Colorado."

As soon as the words left her mouth, she bit her tongue and blushed. She wouldn't be going back to Colorado with Sarah Anne. She would be married and living in the canyon with Joe.

Jacob nodded, his grin perhaps a little wider than before. "Perhaps." Then he rode ahead to catch up with Annabelle.

Elizabeth drew her knees to her chest and looked out over the dark lake capped by the black sky. They had arrived at Lake Tahoe the evening of their second day of traveling, and Joe and Jacob would be leaving in the morning to fetch a preacher from Carson City. In the meantime, Sarah Anne, Annabelle, and Naomi would help her get ready for the marriage ceremony to be held on the shore. Sarah Anne had brought Elizabeth's first mother's wedding dress, which she had hemmed and "fancied-up," as she put it, for Elizabeth.

Tears came to her eyes as she rested her head on her knees, afraid to gaze any longer at the lake—afraid to be reminded of the decision she had made at this very spot months ago, when she had said yes to Joe.

She sensed someone approaching from behind her. Slowly lifting her head, she found Sarah Anne standing nearby.

"Is it all right if I join you?"

She nodded her head, the light from the campfire on the slope enough to illuminate her motions. Sarah Anne sat down beside her. Only distant laughter broke the silence. Elizabeth didn't trust her voice, and she didn't think she could explain her irrational worries to the woman who raised her.

After a while, Sarah Anne asked quietly, "Do you remember Casey?"

"Casey?" Her brows lowered in thought.

"You remember. Louisa and Christy's brother? The two of

you used to chase each other through the fields. He was always bringing you home muddy, your hair in tangles." Sarah Anne chuckled.

Memories flooded her mind, causing tears to burst forth. She did remember Casey, if only barely—more the feeling of contentment than the details themselves. She did recall an afternoon when they'd picked forget-me-nots by the river, and she suddenly ached for those carefree days. Rubbing her palms over her eyes, she finally replied, "I remember. Why'd ya ask?"

Her mother regarded her with a watery blue gaze she couldn't comprehend. "He's alive. Returned home last fall. I saw him before I left on the train."

"Really? But wasn't he…didn't he drown?"

"We all thought so. Apparently he survived, and he's been living in the mountains all this time." Sarah Anne studied her, waiting for something.

"That's wonderful he's alive. His whole family must be so happy, especially after what happened to their pa."

Sarah Anne set a hand on her arm. "Elizabeth, you met him."

"Well, of course, when we were little…" Her words trailed off, and her heartbeat slowed. She recalled hands holding a bunch of flowers out to her, hands that had seemed just big enough and yet gentle enough to encompass the flower stems. A brown gaze that always seemed to melt a little at her gladness, that always sensed her emotions and met them with the response she needed. He hadn't really changed that much, had he?

Her head floated, light and dizzy. "Are you saying that Casey—that Casey is David? That Casey was the one who helped me, the one who…?" She choked on a sob.

Sarah Anne gathered her close as she cried. With a shaky voice, Elizabeth asked, "But how can that be? Why wouldn't he tell me who he was?"

"I don't know, dear. Maybe you should ask him for yourself."

"What?" She pushed back and swiped at her tears with frozen hands.

Her ma's sweet face was silhouetted, but Elizabeth could still see the truth glowing in her eyes. "Casey looked like he would have done just about anything to get on that train with me. He asked me to tell you that he wishes you well, but what he didn't say was just as obvious. He loves you." She paused, searching Elizabeth's eyes in the dim light. "And I think you love him, too."

New, hot tears fell down her cheeks, and she shook her head. "How can you know for sure?"

Sarah Anne smoothed a strand of Elizabeth's hair, brushing her cheek with her thumb. "A mother knows these things, and I had a long train ride to ponder it all. And, dear, ever since I arrived, you've looked rather miserable. Not the attitude of a content and happy soon-to-be bride."

"Oh, Ma." Elizabeth covered her face with her hands. "I can't stop thinking about him. But you don't know the whole story. You don't know about Jacob, or the David I know…"

"No, I don't know. But I do know that Casey's a good man, raised by a good family. One he's chosen to stay with in order to make things right. To help them." She stared up at the sky, where a few stars peeked out from the clouds. "You brought him home."

Homesickness writhed through Elizabeth like a prisoner begging for release. Lifting her gaze to the water—a dark inkwell waiting to be used—she felt her heartbeat quicken. Ever since she had agreed to marry Joe, she'd been caught up in her own emotions. She had been fearful of the future. She had carried bitterness inside her heart toward her own brother. She had forgotten God's tender mercies as she let herself be consumed by her own plans, her own confusion.

160

Grasping her mother's hand, she asked, "Will you please pray with me?"

Joe knew even before Elizabeth approached him at dawn that there would be no wedding. He could feel all his plans and dreams slipping through his fingers like the water he splashed on his face as he sensed her standing behind him, waiting.

"Joe? Can I talk with you?"

He remained crouching by the lake a moment longer, wishing with all his might that he didn't have to hear what she was going to tell him. Finally, he took a deep breath and stood, trying not to clench his fists in anticipation of the anger, shame, and deep sadness he was about to feel.

"Yes, Elizabeth?" With a sudden burst of denial he pushed past her, calling over his shoulder, "We probably shouldn't talk for too long. Me and Jacob have to get to Carson City soon if we want to have the wedding today. Can't have a wedding without a preacher." His attempts at teasing failed miserably, and he knew he sounded just plain ornery. Even now he was losing her, right near where he had first felt the hope of having her forever.

"I...I don't think..."

"If you have somethin' to say, then just come out and tell me straight." Joe turned and crossed his arms over his chest.

Her voice quivered. "I can't marry you." She turned her face away, but not before he saw her eyes fill with moisture.

She sniffed, and he could tell she was about to say more. But he didn't want to hear about David, about how sorry she was, about some false sympathy he didn't need. He shook his head. "I figured as much. Care to tell me why you waited until now to inform me?"

161

Her tears almost softened his resolve, but he wasn't about to open himself up to more heartache when he knew he couldn't win. He should have seen this coming a long time ago.

"I'm so sorry. I didn't know. I didn't realize... I don't belong here." Her words came out confused, as if she were still trying to sort out what she wanted to say. He couldn't wait for her to make sense of her emotions, though. He didn't want to know why he couldn't compete with the likes of David.

"Let's just head back to Virginia City. You can take the train home from there." Swiveling to climb back up the rocky shore, he felt her hand on his arm, restraining him. Heat bloomed from her touch, and when he turned to face her again he met her eyes, green like dew-covered grass. Longing swept over him as suddenly as a piece of chocolate hair fell across her cheek. Swallowing hard, he closed his eyes, the pain of rejection constricting his chest.

"Joe, I'm sorry I've hurt you. You're a good man, and I'm so grateful that you've been watching out for me."

He nodded once and then stepped back out of her reach. She might think him a good man, but somehow he wasn't good enough for her.

Chapter 24

ELIZABETH WAS ALMOST HOME. She gripped Sarah Anne's hand, her gaze landing on Jacob and Annabelle, sitting next to each other across the narrow train aisle. Annabelle's golden head rested on Jacob's chest, and Jacob's arm curled around her shoulders protectively, tenderly. They both appeared to be asleep.

A smile rose on her face as she turned to look back out the window, contentment filling her even as nervousness edged in. The summer green of Colorado blurred as the train sped past, but in her mind Elizabeth could see it clearly—the green hillsides filled with wildflowers, David's cabin surrounded by shimmering aspens, fires brightening the darkness and holding back the night's chill.

Other, darker images marched after. The mountain storm. The creek water closing in over her head. The bear looming over her. David's tears as he confessed what he had almost done in her brother's brothel. Joe's back as he turned away from her when she confessed she couldn't marry him.

She bit her lip, searching the passing landscape for answers. What had been the purpose of knowing Joe if it only ended in his heartbreak? He hadn't even come to see her off at the train station. She didn't blame him.

A welcome peace stole over her, and even though she couldn't explain it, she felt sure that somehow the whole journey had been important, every part. All of those steps had brought her here, and God hadn't abandoned her. In fact, she felt closer to Him now, knowing He had seen the whole landscape and brought her through each trial.

Closing her eyes, she breathed deeply. *Please, dear Lord, bless Joe and his family. Please forgive me for hurting them.*

Her eyes flew open again at the announcement of their arrival in Golden. Anticipation and uncertainty sent fluttery sensations from her belly to her throat. She turned to Sarah Anne. "Would you mind if I went to see him first?"

Sarah Anne shook her head and whispered, "I understand," as she stood to grab their bags from the compartment above their heads. "I'll have Jacob help me bring your things to the house."

"Thank you, Ma." Squeezing into the aisle, she headed for the front of the car.

When the train finally came to a halt, she took one last look back. Bolstered by Sarah Anne's smile, she rushed down the steps. Holding onto her hat, knowing the green ribbons whipped madly behind her, she rushed down the wooden sidewalks of Golden and headed straight out of town. As soon as she passed the last building at the edge of town she ran in earnest. She didn't know what she was going to do when she got to the farm, but there was no room in her heart or mind for anything but the thought of seeing David again.

Stopping for only a moment, she bent to unbutton her feminine boots with trembling fingers. She could run faster without the fancy footwear.

Clutching her boots in one hand and her hat in the other, she flew, heaving in deep gulps of air as the farmhouse finally came into sight. She was about to head to the porch when she saw him. She knew it was him, sitting by the river farther across the property, where they used to play once upon a time.

"David." She called to him, determined to cover the distance between them as quickly as possible, dropping her boots and hat along the way. This time she hoped she would end up in his arms to stay.

Shading his eyes from the sun's glare, David clambered to his feet, sure his heart was deceiving him. Elizabeth would be married to Joe by now, residing in the desert with his family. And yet there was no mistaking the slight frame running straight for him, nor the light brown hair flying behind her.

"Elizabeth?" He barely whispered the word before she was in his arms, the sweet softness of her drowning him in warmth. He clutched her close, nearly afraid to breathe. Was she shaking, or was he?

Pulling back, he framed her face with his hands, searching her gold-green eyes for forgiveness and love. "Elizabeth," he rasped in wonder. "What are you doing here?"

Her chest rose and fell, her eyes aglow and her hair as disheveled as it had been when they'd traversed the Rockies. Finally, she replied between breaths, "We started a journey together, David, or Casey, or whoever you are." She searched his gaze, expectant.

"So we did." His heart soared, then drummed wildly. "But I thought you were going to marry Joe…"

She ducked her head. "I almost did. I thought I could make it work with him, but I was wrong." Peeking up at him, she studied his face. "Is it really you?"

He tucked a strand of hair behind her ear, understanding what she was asking. "Yes. I'm sorry I never told you. I was still coming to terms with my past…"

Before he could explain further, she stood on her tiptoes and brushed a kiss on his cheek, her breath feather-soft. She didn't pull back as she whispered, "Want to know something?"

Oh, yes. "Tell me."

"As Casey, you stole my little heart with your teasing and those forget-me-nots."

He felt the heat of her blush as she lowered her forehead to his shoulder, and he tucked her into his arms, waiting for her to continue.

"As David, you stole my heart again, and I…I want you to keep it."

He couldn't hold back the smile that spread across his face. She was back, back to stay—with him. Releasing her, he bent down and picked a stem of forget-me-nots, the light blue petals bringing back peaceful, precious memories.

Staying down on one knee, he held the stem up to her, relishing the golden glow of the sun surrounding her. "I promise you, with God's help and your permission, I'll take good care of it."

She took the flowers and smiled down at him. As he stood, he drew her into his embrace and basked in the truth of being remembered.

Author's Note

FORGET ME NOT is the story of my heart. Elizabeth and David's journey has been with me for years, and while the details have changed multiple times, the basic plot remains.

I recall one family vacation to Nevada, sitting in a hotel room and jotting down a brief summary as it came to me fast and furious. Everything sort of fell into place, complete with a desert setting that had intrigued me, and all tied together with forget-me-not stems. I certainly had a long road ahead of me before FORGET ME NOT was ready for publication, but the heart of the story beat steady from its birth.

Through my high school years, I worked on the book in fits and starts. (There was even a contemporary version—more along the lines of *The Journey of Natty Gann*, a movie I love with a hero I adore—but with some encouragement from my dad and a passion for all things American West, the story ended up as a Western, thank goodness!) When it came time to choose a topic for an extended essay I had to write for the International Baccalaureate Diploma Programme, I picked my book's main setting, Virginia City. That decision led to another trip to the tourist town in the hills above Reno the summer before my senior year of high school, which caused my family and me to fall more in love with the town…which subsequently led to more trips. We still haven't been able to get enough of the place!

During our visits we stayed first at the Seven Mile Canyon Guest Ranch—the area where I set the fictional Clifton ranch—and then Edith Palmer's Country Inn. Little tidbits I learned from the owners of those B&Bs and other locals fed my imagination, which is how I ended up including such things as a Cornish character who stole my heart (and who plans to be the hero of Book 3), a

Jewish wife for Seth, and yellow roses. As for some fact vs. fiction, note that the Delta and the Bucket of Blood were and are actual establishments in Virginia City, whereas Jacob's businesses are fictional (although D Street did indeed have a red-light district).

It wasn't until my second year of college that I finally completed the novel. As soon as I wrote "The End," I was beyond ready to share it with the world. The only problem? I may have been ready (or at least I thought I was), but my story was not. It took some helpful (yet still encouraging) feedback from author friends for me to realize that FORGET ME NOT needed to be pruned and trimmed before it could fully bloom. So I put aside my query attempts and moved on to write the sequel, BLEEDING HEART.

Two years later, I felt that BLEEDING HEART, while certainly not perfect, was ready. I had grown in the interim—met some people, learned of some publishing possibilities, and found myself in a new place where editing a story and making it better wasn't so daunting of a task. And that's why the second book in this series was published first.

Every story has a season, and FORGET ME NOT has its turn to blossom now. As the foundation for the series, providing back story for certain characters and exploring themes very close to my heart, I had to return to it. If you read BLEEDING HEART first, I hope that the characters' histories endeared them more to you and answered some questions their words in the sequel might have raised. If this is your first experience with "The Heart's Spring" series, I hope you enjoy revisiting some of these characters in Book 2!

If you'd like to learn more about FORGET ME NOT, please visit *www.ForgetMeNotNovel.blogspot.com*. For all the latest news about this book series, be sure to also check out the series blog at *www.TheHeartsSpringSeries.blogspot.com*.

Discussion Questions

1. Have you ever been given a startling revelation regarding your family or a friend's past? How did you respond? If you were faced with a similar situation again, would you react differently?

2. How did you feel about Jacob and Annabelle? Did your feelings change toward them as the story progressed?

3. Was there ever a point when you wanted Elizabeth to marry Joe instead of David? What do you think caused Elizabeth to choose David in the end?

4. Which setting did you prefer to read about—the Rocky Mountains of Colorado or Virginia City?

   What did you like about each setting, and how did each leg of the journey present different challenges to the characters?

5. Have you ever felt forgotten by God? What tender mercies have you been shown that remind you that you're remembered?

Acknowledgements

The process of writing FORGET ME NOT was a long one, but some wonderful people came along and made the journey exciting, enjoyable, and unforgettable. I was blessed by each person who took the time to listen to me ramble on about the story, to share their advice and knowledge with me, and to show me that this was a dream worth holding onto.

Heartfelt thanks to…

MY FAMILY. You've given me the love and means to write my stories, and I can't thank you enough for all that you do. To my mom—thank you for sharing precious moments and memories with me, for always taking the time to show you care. And to my sister, Emily—thank you for letting me use your middle name and pick your brain about horses. Your talents are inspiring, Ems, so keep on dreaming big!

ADRIENNE HEDLUND, ELENA LOPEZ, and HANNAH DAWLEY, three of the dearest friends a girl could ask for. Thank you for all of the writing encouragement, but most importantly, for just being there through it all. Love you!

AMANDA STANLEY. This season came, dear friend! Thank you for believing it would in God's timing, and for making the latter half of the writing process so much fun. Your friendship is a true blessing.

ELIZABETH LUDWIG. Your feedback on my first draft was invaluable, and I can't tell you how much you've helped me grow as a writer. Thank you for taking me under your wing.

LAURA FRANTZ. You have always been so encouraging, from your endorsement on my imaginary press release three years ago, to your endorsement for my real debut. I'm so honored by your thoughtfulness, and I deeply admire your work and joyful attitude.

LENA GOLDFINCH. You showed me that self-publishing is not only a viable route, but also an exciting and rewarding one. You've been an amazing example to me, but what's more, you've been an incredibly generous mentor, an absolutely awesome cover designer, and a wonderful friend. I'm so grateful to know you and work with you.

RACHELLE REA, my editing buddy and blogging friend! I'm so glad to have you as my proofreader. Your kindness, skill, and profound insight mean more than you know.

ONCE AGAIN, TO MY VIRGINIA CITY FRIENDS: Leisa Findley (Edith Palmer's Country Inn), Gary and Nancy Teel (TNT Stagelines), Judy Sorensen, Karen Tassone, Desna Young, and Joe Curtis (Mark Twain Bookstore). Here's the book that started it all, and it includes a little more of the town I've come to know and love. Thank you for helping me with my research and making Virginia City's history come to life for me!

MY TWITTER WRITING BUDDIES. Rewrites and edits went much faster thanks to you! I greatly appreciate the extra motivation, and I had a blast sharing favorite lines and knowing I wasn't staring at a computer screen alone.

MY INFLUENCER TEAM. To all those awesome blogging friends who have helped me to spread the word about my books, encouraging me in so many ways and taking the time to write reviews (and so much more)—my sincere gratitude. Your enthusiasm and support mean the world to me!

MY GRANDMA'S ART CLASS. You celebrated my debut with me and my grandma, and you brought joy to us both. Thank you for being there for all of us.

Other Books in
"The Heart's Spring" Series

BLEEDING HEART
(Book 2)

A desperate soiled dove. Three men who come to care for her. One man determined to claim her.

All on a journey that will show them what true love really involves.

Now available in paperback and Kindle e-book formats.

MORNING GLORY
(Book 3)

Myghal's story continues...
Summer 2014

About the Author

AMBER STOKES has a Bachelor of Science degree in English and a passion for the written word—from blogging to writing poetry, short stories, and novels. After her brief time at college in Oregon, she is now back home among the redwoods of Northern California, living life one day at a time and pursuing her passion for books via freelance editing and self-publishing.

She loves to meet new reader and writer friends! You can connect with Amber on her blog, SEASONS OF HUMILITY, as well as on Twitter, Pinterest, and Goodreads. You can also drop her a line at amberstokes@corban.edu.

Word-of-mouth can be crucial to a new author's success.
If you enjoyed this book, please consider leaving a review online.

Thank you!